AMISH CHRISTMAS TREASURE

TWO AMISH CHRISTMAS NOVELLAS

RACHEL J. GOOD

NO ROOM AT THE INN

CHAPTER ONE

Gusts of wind sliced through Philip Troyer's coat and pants. Snow stung his face. About a mile ago, his fingers had frozen into place gripping the handlebars of his scooter despite his thick gloves. Then the motor sputtered and died. He'd run out of gas.

It didn't matter. The scooter never could have gotten through the country lane he'd just turned onto. The road had iced over, and drifts blocked his way ahead. Why hadn't he listened to the guys at the firehouse and spent the night? As usual, he'd been stubborn. And determined nothing would stop him.

And it hadn't. Not for the first three miles. But if he didn't get somewhere warm soon, his toes and fingers would be frostbitten.

All the farmhouses he passed had their lights out, and they were high on hills, much too far from the road. Suppose he slogged up the long driveways only to find nobody home? Better to keep going.

A dim light shone ahead. A star in the sky? A mirage? He

trudged toward the beacon, hoping, praying it signaled a place to stop.

As he drew closer, the star on the roof of the Dutch Valley Inn flickered faintly through the blinding storm. Half pushing-half carrying his scooter, he struggled the last quarter mile through the ever-deepening snow.

As he tromped through huge frosted ice piles blocking the motel driveway, he passed a neon sign to the left almost buried in the snow. *No Vacancy*, it said. So, no room at the inn tonight.

That didn't matter. He didn't have enough money for a room. If he could make it to the front door, maybe he could shelter in the lobby. He hoped they wouldn't mind if he sat on one of their couches until he thawed out enough to trek the last two miles home. *If I manage to stumble the rest of the way to the door, that is.*

~

After dropping off an armload of fresh towels to one of the rooms, Katie Stoltzfus inhaled deeply as she neared the motel lobby. The crisp, clean scent of the fifteen-feet tall balsam fir perfumed the air. Lights twinkled between the silver bows, white doves, and burgundy balls decorating the branches.

Although Katie's Amish family Christmas never included a tree or even greenery during the holiday season, the sight of this loveliness lifted her spirits. Her family preferred their faith and spirituality simple and unadorned. But for Katie, this beauty made her heart swell. It reminded her of God's creation and his bounty.

Nearby, gas logs burned in the two-sided glass-fronted fireplace. Although the lobby with its high ceilings was huge and held assorted seating areas, the fire and the tree made it seem cozy and homey. Outside the windows, snow pelted down, but inside, the flames gave off comforting warmth.

Three young brothers, unaccompanied by an adult, wrestled each other on the couch near the tree. The oldest one had the middle boy in a headlock, while the youngest jumped on his back.

"Leave Jake alone!" the little one shouted, trying to pull his big brother away.

Katie rushed toward them to prevent someone from getting hurt. If she'd been less shy, she might have yelled. But she rarely spoke above a whisper. They'd never hear her.

She was too late. The largest boy rippled his shoulder muscles, dislodging his youngest brother, who tumbled into the Christmas tree.

Crash! Three glass balls smashed onto the floor, sending shards spraying in all directions.

The sudden noise stopped the fight. The oldest boy shot to his feet and whirled around.

The middle brother wriggled free and ran down the hall, yelling, "Mom, Carter's beating on me again."

But the youngest boy sat stunned amid the wreckage, his blond hair tangled in tree branches, his fists scrubbing at his eyes as he wailed, "It's. . . your. . . fault, Carter."

"It's all right," Katie assured him when she was near enough for him to hear. "It was an accident. I'll clean it up."

A tired, dishwater blonde stuck her head into the hallway. "Carter Jones, get in here right now."

Carter gulped, reached down, yanked his little brother to his feet, ignoring the small boy's cries of pain as strands of his hair stuck to needle-covered branches.

"Wait," Katie said softly. She stepped over and untangled each clump of hair and brushed off pine needles while Carter huffed impatiently and bounced on his toes.

The minute Katie set the youngest boy free, Carter dragged his brother down the hall.

Katie shook her head. They'd been here three weeks now,

and she had no idea how long they'd be staying. Every day, though, they created disturbances or broke things or spilled drinks. Katie cleaned up after them without complaint. Just like she was doing now as she headed to the cleaning closet for a broom and dustpan.

Her heart went out to their mom, who'd run from an abusive boyfriend. When she'd arrived, wearing only a robe and slippers in the middle of the night, trailed by three sniffling sons in pajamas, she'd had bruises on her arms and face. The marks had slowly faded to purple and yellow. Most were almost gone, but the marks on her spirit hadn't lessened. Her eyes still held a desperate, hunted look. Katie prayed for the mother and boys every day but wished she could find a way to help.

Her manager, Anand, had given the woman a low monthly room rate. He had a soft heart, and because his dad owned the inn, he could make decisions like that. But even that amount had been hard on the woman.

Since she'd arrived, she'd struggled to find a job. Katie pitied all four of them cramped in a hotel room over Christmas. The boys wouldn't have a family holiday. And one day last week, when Katie went in to change the bed linens, their mom had been crying because she couldn't afford to buy them any Christmas gifts.

After Katie got home that night, she told *Mamm*, and since then, all her sisters had helped to gather a few toys and books. Katie had also spent the past few days baking and decorating homemade cookies for everyone who'd be stuck here far from home this holiday weekend. She'd packaged them in pretty bags with bows—enough for each room and all the staff—and filled an extra basketful after the weatherman predicted a terrible snowstorm.

Usually, the inn stayed quiet this time of year, but with the Holiday Extravaganza in town this past week plus the blizzard that had blown in yesterday and continued unabated today, many tourists had ended up stuck here until the plows cleared the roads. On back country roads like this, crews rarely came through. Most guests were far from home, and Katie wanted each one to have a special Christmas.

As she swept the bits of broken Christmas balls into the dustpan, snow came down even harder outside. Drifts accumulated against the glass entrance doors, and a curtain of snow blocked visibility.

She wondered if her youth group had gone caroling tonight. If they had, everyone had gathered at the Kings' house by now for hot chocolate and cookies. Part of Katie wished she'd gone with them instead of volunteering to work the overnight shift on Christmas Eve, but most of the other staff had children. So, Katie had offered to work so they could spend time with their families.

Besides, she wasn't sure she could keep a cheerful smile pasted on her face while her best friend, Leanne, spent all her time with her boyfriend. Now that Leanne had announced her engagement, she barely had time for Katie, who watched the romance from afar, feeling lonely and adrift.

As the only one of her buddy bunch still unattached, Katie often felt like a third wheel. She could hang around some of the younger girls, but that only made her feel more left out. The boy Katie had dreamed of dating had married someone else in November, making it painful for her to watch all the paired-off couples, their faces and eyes glowing, flashing each other secret smiles.

Working on Christmas Eve wasn't much better. Instead of going home to be with her family, Katie would sleep in the last available motel bedroom after her shift ended tonight. Then she'd be up early to prepare the continental breakfast buffet tomorrow.

She'd thought being here and staying busy might ease some

of her loneliness, but it wasn't working. Because here she was . . . picking up pieces of shattered Christmas balls like bits of her broken life.

~

Philip focused on the star as he pushed his exhausted muscles through the drifts. As he neared the door, the light glowing inside the lobby caught his attention. The driving snow obscured his vision, but he could make out a pretty Amish girl in a green dress, sweeping. He wasn't sure if the flurrying flakes stinging his eyes were making her appear sad or if she had tears on her cheeks. It hurt his heart to see an Amish girl working on Christmas Eve. She should be home with her family.

By concentrating on her, he powered through the last few feet to the sidewalk, which had recently been shoveled, but the blizzard had already coated the walkway with several more inches. Philip propped his scooter against the brick wall near the entrance. An awning covered the front door and driveway, providing some protection from the storm's fury, but layers of ice had frozen against the lobby door. He had to pull hard and drag the heavy door through the packed snow and ice.

He stumbled into the lobby, exhausted. Warmth seeped through his clothes. And his fingers, toes, and face prickled and burned.

The girl looked up, startled. She had been crying. Traces of tears still sparkled on her cheeks. She held a dustpan filled with broken Christmas balls. And she seemed wary, as if his appearance frightened her. Then she glanced toward the front desk.

A soft *ach* fell from her lips. And in a voice barely above a whisper, she said, "I'm sorry. Anand went to change a light bulb. He'll be right back."

Philip had no idea who Anand was. Perhaps the desk clerk? "It's all right. If I could warm up by the fire for a while, I'll be on my way."

Alarm filled her eyes. "You shouldn't be out in weather like this. Why don't you stay overnight?"

Philip's lips quirked. "You mean in the lobby?" They'd let him sleep here?

"*Neh*, in a room."

"*Danke*, but I can't afford that. Besides, I saw the *No Vacancy* sign out front."

"We have one room reserved for staff. You can stay there for free."

"But what about the staff?"

"No one will be sleeping there tonight."

"If you're sure?"

At her nod, relief coursed through him. He'd pulled a double shift at the fire station to fill in for someone who'd been snowed in. Then they'd battled a blaze for hours and barely made it back to the station on the icy roads. Rather than resting, he'd helped shovel out the station's parking lot. When a plow went through an hour before his second shift ended, he decided to make it home. It was either that or sleep on the firehouse floor. He'd been on his feet for hours and had barely staggered in here after battling the snow.

"A room would be wonderful."

Maybe after the storm abated, he could return and offer to pay for the room. A hot shower and clean bed sounded like heaven. Speaking of heaven, this Amish girl appeared angelic with firelight and tree lights flickering behind her. Or maybe his gratitude had colored her beautiful. He gave the girl a brilliant smile.

Her eyes widened, and she dropped her gaze. She seemed as skittish as a colt. Her voice still quiet, but much more formal, she said, "Let me show you to your room."

"I really appreciate this. I can come by to pay after the storm lets up."

"No need. The room really is free."

"If you're sure?"

"I am." Her firm words stopped any further argument. She reached into her pocket and handed him a key card. "I'll show you to the room."

They'd started toward the hallway, when a man emerged from the opposite hallway and slipped behind the front desk, whistling a Christmas tune.

Katie stiffened and stopped walking. "Anand, I—"

The lobby door burst open. A man lurched through the door, looking on the point of collapse.

"I need help. My car's stuck."

All Philip wanted was that hot shower and a warm bed. He didn't relish going out into the storm. But he could never turn down anyone in need.

CHAPTER TWO

The man's voice, tight and desperate, begged for immediate assistance. "We're on the way to the hospital, and the car spun out. The front end's stuck in a snowbank. My wife's in the car."

"Can you watch the desk, Katie?" Anand rushed around the counter. "I don't think we'll be getting any visitors tonight, but some of our guests may need assistance."

Katie froze. He'd never asked her to work behind the counter before. She'd been grateful to do housekeeping behind the scenes and not have to interact much with customers.

What if the phone rang? Would she have to answer it? She had trouble talking to people in person, but her phone phobia was even worse. She always panicked as she strained to carry on a conversation with a disembodied voice.

Before she could squeak out an excuse, Anand grabbed two shovels from the utility closet and raised his eyebrows at Philip. "You willing to help?" When Philip nodded, Anand handed Philip a bucket of salt.

"Maybe we could use the rubber mat by the door to put

under the wheels." Philip glanced at Anand with a question in his eyes.

"Good idea." Anand nodded to the *Englischer*. "Why don't you take that?"

The man stopped wringing his hands together to pick up the mat. "Hurry, please hurry. We need to get to the hospital."

Philip shook his head. "Most of the roads haven't been plowed. I'm not sure you can get through."

Desperation shone in the man's eyes. "But I have to. My wife—"

"Is she hurt? How bad is it? I work at the firehouse and have some EMT training. Maybe I can help?"

Katie's heart fluttered. The handsome stranger was the nicest man she'd ever met. A firefighter. He'd been so worn out when he came through the door, she couldn't let him walk back out into the Arctic temperatures. She'd felt compelled to offer him her room. And now, instead of collapsing into bed, which he sorely needed, he'd offered to assist someone else.

∾

Philip rushed toward the door as he waited for an answer. If they'd been headed to the hospital, there was no time to waste.

The man's pinched face contrasted with the pride in his eyes. "She's having a baby."

A lump rose in Philip's throat, and he swallowed hard. He had no idea how to deliver a baby. But the woman needed help. She and her husband would never make it to the hospital in this weather.

Philip didn't hesitate. "You'd better bring her in here." Not knowing how to do something never stopped him before.

"You can deliver babies?"

"I'll call the firehouse and have them talk me through it."

The terror in the man's eyes increased. "You don't know how to do it."

"They have ambulances at the firehouse. We'll have them send one." Philip used the authoritative voice he'd perfected when he had to order gawkers back from a fire. It calmed his own nerves and assured others around him he knew exactly what he was doing—even if he didn't.

Philip didn't add that the roads were much too treacherous for the ambulance to get here unless a snowplow came through first. But maybe a miracle might happen.

The man's fingers dug into Philip's arm. "It's our first baby. I want everything to go right."

"It will." Philip stated that with a confidence he didn't feel. But babies came into the world all the time. It had to be a pretty natural process. At least, he hoped that was true.

A short while later, the man supported his wife into the lobby. She groaned and doubled over in the entranceway. Sweat beaded on her forehead despite the frigid air blowing through the open door.

"We don't have an open room unless. . ." Anand lifted his eyes to Katie.

Helplessly, she turned to Philip. "I gave the key to, um . . ."

"Philip," he supplied. "That was your room?"

"Jah."

How generous she'd been. She looked as tired as he felt. But right now, someone else needed that room more than either of them.

Philip answered her unspoken question, "Of course, she can have the room."

Anand stared from one to the other. "You gave up your room, Katie?"

Without answering, she slid from behind the desk. "It's Room 112. I'll show you the way."

Philip handed her the key card and trailed them down the hall.

"I can't afford to pay," the man said as they stopped for a moment while his wife had a contraction.

"The room's free," Philip assured him. "It's a staff room."

"You are sure?"

Philip nodded, and a few of the lines on the man's face relaxed. The father-to-be had enough to worry about without the added concern of paying. Philip was grateful he could reassure the man about one thing. If they owed money, Philip would stop by the day after Christmas to pay. But what had he gotten himself into with offering to deliver a baby?

∾

Katie stood rigid behind the desk, praying all would go well for the couple stuck in the snow. And praying almost equally as hard the phone wouldn't ring. It hadn't. That had been a miracle. And now Katie was praying for this poor young mother, so tired, drained, and frightened.

For once, Katie was in her element. She ushered everyone into Room 112. "I'll get rubber sheeting for the bed, fresh bedding, and towels," she said shyly.

She didn't know a lot about delivering babies, but she could make the woman comfortable.

A short while later, she returned with a cart full of clean towels, extra bedding, and two rubberized pads they put under the bedsheets. Her fingers deft, she stripped the bed, added a double layer of mattress pads and remade the bed.

She met the woman's grateful eyes. "There you go."

With her husband assisting, the woman climbed into the bed. Despite the sweat running down her face, she was shivering. Katie covered her with a blanket, and Philip thanked her with his eyes before talking to the woman, and Katie's heart danced.

He reached into his pocket and pulled out his cell phone. "Oh great, it's dead. Either of you have a phone?"

Diego shook his head.

"Katie?"

She started when Philip called her name. How did he know it? Oh, *jah*, Anand had used it, but hearing it from Philip's lips did strange things to her insides.

Katie scolded herself. Right now, they needed to concentrate on this young mother. Besides, never again would Katie allow herself to pine for someone who barely knew she existed. And Philip would be gone after today. Katie had learned her lesson about letting her heart get involved. Nobody would want a wife as shy and mousy as she was.

Still, she couldn't help admiring Philip's competence and take-charge attitude. She'd been so busy staring at him, she hadn't realized he'd said her name a second time.

"*Jah?*"

"You have a cell?" When she shook her head, Philip frowned down at the buttons on the tan phone on the bedside table. "Is there any way to put this on speaker?"

"I don't know." She'd never had any reason to check. She wiped the phones off when she cleaned the rooms, but she'd never examined the buttons.

He'd picked up the phone and held out the receiver. Her heart dropped. The block in her throat scooted its way to her stomach, which tightened into knots. She stared at the phone. *Neh*, please don't ask me.

But Philip didn't hear her silent plea. He thrust the receiver into her hand. "If you can hold it to my ear while I get— I'm sorry. I don't know your name." He glanced at the woman, but her husband answered.

15

"Isabella," her husband answered. "Isabella Garcia. And I'm Diego."

Philip nodded. "Nice to meet you. I'm Philip Troyer." He turned his attention back to the wife. "Could you scoot down a bit, Isabella?"

Katie stood there, shaking, staring at the receiver in her hands.

Philip turned back to her. "I'm going to wash up. I won't want to touch the phone after that. I'll talk to them at the station, but after that, you'll need to tell me what he says. And ask my questions."

Instruct a strange man in this room and talk to another one on the phone? Please, God, find another volunteer. When Moses begged, You sent Aaron in his place.

But by the time Philip returned from the bathroom, no substitute appeared to take her place.

~

"Dial this number." Philip rattled off the number of the fire station.

She cringed and fumbled with the phone. He regretted being so brusque. He'd only meant to be efficient. Usually, he barked orders at the guys during fires and other emergencies. They all did. It helped them get the job done, and no one took offense.

He hadn't meant to scare her. She looked frightened to death. He softened his tone and repeated the number slowly this time.

His quieter voice didn't change her *deer-in-the-headlights* look. Maybe she was worried about the mother-to-be.

"Everything will be all right," he assured her and everyone else, including himself.

Her fingers shook as she punched in the numbers.

"Can you hold the phone to my ear while I explain?"

Some of the distress lines on her face smoothed out, but the phone still trembled while she pressed it to his ear. Because of nervousness or from being so close to him?

Philip relaxed a bit when his friend Deshawn's cheery voice flowed over the line. "Hey, man, you made it home already? We've been worried about you."

"I'm not home. I'm at the Dutch Valley Inn." Although it was a long shot, Philip had to ask. "Any chance you could get an ambulance out here? A woman's having a baby."

Deshawn hesitated. "We've gotten almost a foot of snow since you left, and the plow hasn't come by. The chief called for one, but they're not sure how long it'll take. We'll come as soon as we can. Meanwhile, you're on your own."

"But I've nev—" Philip stopped himself before he reminded everyone in the room he'd never delivered a baby. He needed to instill confidence in them, convince them he was capable.

"You can do it, buddy." Deshawn had picked up on Philip's fears. "You grew up on a farm. You must have had some livestock, right? Didn't you help with some of those deliveries?"

Phillip swallowed hard. "*Jah.*"

"Hand the phone to someone and get to work," Deshawn ordered. "I'll talk you through everything. It'll be fine."

Philip turned to Katie. "Can you listen and repeat the instructions?"

That same fearful expression filled her face. Was she worried he couldn't handle this?

"It'll be all right," he soothed, but that didn't seem to help.

He didn't blame her. He'd already admitted he'd never delivered a baby. And although Deshawn had reminded Philip that he'd helped calves and lambs into the world, that had been years ago. Would delivering a human baby be similar? He only prayed there'd be no complications.

17

CHAPTER THREE

$\mathcal{K}$atie clenched the phone and prayed for courage. Then, her gaze landed on the woman lying on the bed.

Her conscience jagged her. *Why are you so worried about yourself when you should be thinking about Isabella's welfare?*

I'm sorry, Lord. Please protect Isabella and help her to have a healthy baby. And give me the strength to repeat all the instructions and ask the needed questions.

Katie caught Diego's eye and motioned to the ice bucket near the bed. "Maybe sucking on some ice chips would help? And a cool washcloth for her forehead?"

"Great idea," a voice boomed in her ear.

She jumped. She'd forgotten she was holding the receiver.

"You talking to the baby's dad?" the man on the phone asked.

"J-Jah."

"Good. He can help too. When she's ready to push, have him get behind her back and hold her."

"A-All right."

"What'd he say?" Philip looked at her with an expectant

expression. He must have thought she'd gotten instructions for him.

Her voice quavering, Katie repeated the suggestion.

Diego nodded. "I will do that. We did take childbirth classes. I'm glad you reminded me of this, Katie." He placed an ice chip in Isabella's mouth, and she glanced up at him with love and gratitude, a look he returned.

Katie wished someday a man would stare at her like that.

"By the way, his name's Deshawn." Philip gestured to the phone. Then he yelled, "Deshawn, you're talking to Katie."

"Gotcha," the deep voice came over the phone line. "Nice to meet you, Katie."

"Same here," she said weakly. Inside, she was sweating as much as Isabella.

For the next half hour, she relayed Deshawn's commands and Philip's questions. Isabella had just transitioned to pushing when Deshawn whooped. Katie almost dropped the phone.

"The plow's here," he shouted loudly enough for everyone in the room to hear. "We'll head to the inn, but I'll get on my cell so I can keep contact."

Philip cheered, and Katie managed to dial the number to switch to Deshawn's cell despite sweaty palms. To place a phone call twice in one day unnerved her, but she'd done it. And actually, it hadn't been the same day. The bedside clock had ticked past midnight while she dialed.

"Merry Christmas," Deshawn said as he picked up Katie's call.

Diego smoothed his wife's hair back from her forehead with a cool washcloth. "We're going to have a Christmas baby."

She smiled faintly, then closed her eyes, and panted through a contraction.

On the phone, Deshawn talked them through the crowning.

"After that," he said, "the baby should slide out easily. Wrap it in a clean blanket."

A clean blanket? Katie should have thought of that. But they didn't have any small enough for a baby. For the first time that night, she had a question of her own. "A pillowcase or towel?" She'd been thinking to herself. She hadn't meant to say that aloud, but Deshawn answered.

"Of course. Anything soft and clean will work."

The hotel towels were rough and scratchy. Katie took several of the softest pillowcases from the cart.

A loud cry interrupted her. She whirled around.

"It's a boy," Philip shouted.

"Congratulations!" Deshawn yelled back. "We're only a few minutes away. We can handle cutting the cord." He clicked off.

Katie dropped the receiver and hurried over with the pillowcases. She wrapped the precious baby in two pillowcases and wiped each delicate feature with another one before handing him to his mother.

Isabella stared down at her son with tears in her eyes. "He's beautiful."

"He is, and so are you." Diego moved from behind to sit next to her. He wrapped an arm around his wife and touched his son's cheek with a gentle finger.

Katie watched them with a lump in her throat.

Isabella beamed. "It is Christmas, *si?* I know what we should name him. *Jesús.*" She pronounced it *Hay-soos* and looked to her husband for approval.

Diego nodded. "*Perfecto.* In honor of our Lord. Today is His birthday." He smiled at her. "And he's even wrapped in swaddling clothes like the Savior."

Isabella's face creased into a worried frown. "We do have some baby things in the car."

"I'll go out and get them for you," Philip volunteered, "as soon as the ambulance crew arrives."

Though his face was wreathed with smiles, he appeared exhausted. He'd been tired when he arrived. Katie worried he might keel over. She couldn't believe all he'd done to help bring this tiny baby into the world. What a Christmas miracle!

The door to the lobby banged open, and several people tramped down the hallway to the room.

"It's this room," Anand said outside the door. Then he knocked.

"Come in," Philip called.

Deshawn entered first, a wide smile stretching his face. "You did it, bro!"

A woman followed him into the room and headed straight for the baby. "I'll check the Apgar score and cut the cord." She bustled over to the bed, and murmuring in a low voice, she spoke to the new parents and cared for the baby.

Katie needed to clean up the room and change the bedding, but maybe she could slip out now while everyone was occupied. She edged toward the door, but Deshawn stopped her.

"You must be Katie." He stuck out a hand to shake and pumped hers up and down vigorously. "You're as much of a hero as my man here." He waved toward Philip. "The two of you did an awesome job. Great teamwork."

~

Filled with gratitude the ordeal had ended well, Philip stretched and yawned. The bed he'd hoped to sleep on now held a family of three. Since the plow had come through, perhaps he could make it the last few miles to his *onkel*'s home.

He hadn't properly thanked Katie, but first he needed to wash up. He slipped into the bathroom while Deshawn had Katie trapped, regaling her with the tale of the fire they'd put out earlier—or rather yesterday, since it was now well after midnight.

When he came back out, Katie turned wide eyes to him, her

face filled with awe. "I can't believe you saved a little girl, put out a fire, and delivered a baby all in the same day."

Her quiet voice did strange things to his insides. So did gazing into the green depths of her lovely eyes.

Deshawn cleared his throat. "I'll leave you two alone."

"What?" Philip shook himself free from the spell of Katie's eyes. "I'll help you do whatever else needs to be done."

"Naw, man." Deshawn clapped him on the shoulder. "You've done enough for one day. Go rest."

"If you don't need me, I guess I'll be going. Now that the plow cleared the road, I can get home."

"You nuts?" Deshawn shot him an incredulous look. "The temperature's dropped below zero, and the wind chill makes it even worse."

Katie's gentle voice stopped him. "It's not safe to be out in this weather. I'd worry about you getting home. A couch isn't the most comfortable place to sleep, but I can fix it up with bedding and blankets."

How could he say *nah* to her kind offer? Besides, he'd like to get to know her better. And his exhaustion had gone bone deep. But he didn't want to put her out or make her work long hours.

"Hasn't your shift ended? I don't want you to go to extra trouble."

"Not yet. And I still have to clean up in here." She waved a hand toward the bed. "It would be no trouble." She ducked her head. "I like doing it."

He believed her. Sincerity oozed from her words. Like him, she liked to serve and help people.

"I didn't thank you yet for your assistance. I couldn't have done it without you. "

She kept her head lowered. "I didn't do anything. You and Deshawn did it all."

Deshawn shook his head at the same time Philip contradicted her. "How would I have heard the instructions without you?"

Her cheeks pinkened, and she appeared ready to protest.

He cut it off. "*Danke* for what you did."

Philip could barely hear her "You're welcome."

That piqued his curiosity. Why did such a charming girl speak so softly, as if her words weren't important and neither was she? That bothered him. He'd stay the night just to have a chance to ask her that question.

Katie squirmed under his scrutiny. He hadn't meant to make her uncomfortable. He seemed to do that a lot.

Her movements tense, she turned and headed for the door. "I'll go fix your bed." She scurried off before he could stop her again.

Anand motioned to Philip's clothing. "You're a mess. You can use the shower in my quarters. And I'll lend you some clothes. Katie can wash those for you."

"I don't want her to do that."

"It's no trouble. Katie doesn't mind. She'll have to clean up in here anyway. I'll be paying her overtime."

Philip was grateful for a change of clothes, even if they weren't Amish. But he didn't want to add to Katie's workload. He'd take the borrowed clothes home and wash and return them tomorrow.

When he emerged fresh from the shower and in the sweatsuit Anand had lent him, Philip balled up his clothes and headed for the lobby.

Katie had spread out fresh linens on the couch closest to the fire. She'd piled a few pillows at terminate and added several blankets and a duvet. In a back corner of the room, tucked away in a nook, she'd made a bed for herself.

She did a double take when she saw him.

"Anand suggested I borrow some clothes." Philip gave her a rueful smile. "Your boss probably didn't want me to dirty those nice white sheets." With his bundle of clothes, he gestured toward the comfy couch she'd prepared.

Katie reached out for the clothes in his hands. "I'll wash those when I do Isabella's sheets."

Philip held them out of reach. "You've done enough tonight. I can wash these at home and bring Anand's sweatsuit back tomorrow."

She bit her lips. From what he'd seen of her so far, she didn't like to argue or assert herself. But she surprised him by standing on tiptoe and snatching the balled-up clothing from his hand.

That took him by surprise. So did the sparks that shot through him at her touch. He released his grip, and a small, triumphant smile crossed her face.

"I'll get them back to you in the morning. Now I need to go collect Isabella's sheets." Her head held a little higher and her steps almost jaunty, she headed down the hall.

A few minutes ago, Philip had been so weary he'd been fighting to keep his eyes open. But the encounter with Katie had energized him. Her soft fingers had ignited every nerve ending in his body. He wanted to spend time with her and get to know her. He'd never felt such a deep longing, a magnetic pull he couldn't fight.

CHAPTER FOUR

*K*atie practically bounced down the hall with Philip's clothes in her hands. She couldn't believe she'd been bold enough to reach up and grab them from him. What had she been thinking?

Rather than embarrassing her, that out-of-character behavior filled Katie with elation. Within the past few hours, she'd done two things she never would have attempted before —talking on the phone and contradicting someone and taking something out of that person's hand. Actually, make that— three things. She'd also engaged in conversation—and a little teasing—with an Amish man instead of ducking her head and avoiding him.

Philip hadn't put up much of fight. Most likely, she wouldn't have persisted if he had. But she was grateful for her small victory.

Mamm would be shocked if she'd seen Katie tonight. And for some reason, Katie doubted she'd share this small incident. For the past few years, *Mamm* had been trying to get Katie to come out of her shell. She wouldn't consider grabbing something out of a man's hands a good way to do that.

Her mother had been the one who'd pushed Katie to apply to work at the front desk. Unlike her older sisters, Katie had always been shy and tongue-tied around people. Luckily, Anand also needed housekeepers, which suited Katie perfectly. Katie loved helping people, but she'd rather do it behind the scenes. She'd been grateful she'd never had to work behind the front desk before tonight.

She found herself humming as she entered Room 112 after knocking. Diego was helping Isabella take a shower, and the EMT who'd taken care of the newborn was sitting in a chair, cradling the baby. The infant had been cleaned, tucked into a sleeper, and wrapped in a blanket.

Philip must have gone out to the car to retrieve the baby clothes. Katie hadn't seen him do that, which surprised her because she seemed to be hyperaware of his presence. Perhaps he'd done it while she'd made up his bed.

What a kind man he was! He'd followed Anand out the door to help Diego with the snowbound car. He'd given up his room and his sleep to help deliver a baby. And he'd been gentle when Katie fumbled the phone call. If it weren't for his reassuring glance, she'd never have been able to relay Deshawn's messages.

"I'm just collecting the sheets," Katie told the EMT, who nodded without looking up from the baby.

Katie bundled up the bedding and stuffed it into a clean trash bag tied to the cart. Then she sanitized her hands and remade the bed with fresh linens. She'd just finished when Diego assisted Isabella back into the room. Her face tired but glowing, Isabella wore a pretty nightgown and had her hair wrapped in a towel.

"Oh, you've cleaned everything." She flashed Katie a grateful smile.

"Thank you so much." Diego's formal tone contrasted with his broad grin. "We can't thank you and Philip enough for all you've done." His gaze moved to the EMT. "And both of you. God has blessed us tonight."

"As if the gift of His Son wasn't already enough," Isabella added.

Katie praised the Lord for both Christmas births. The spirit of thankfulness stayed with her as she soaked the sheets to remove the stains and tossed Philip's clothes into another washer with some of the darks she needed to launder. When both washers had been filled and turned on, she slipped into the kitchen to do some prep work for the next morning's breakfast. She wanted it to be special.

By the time Philip's laundry was done, Katie was exhausted. She carried his clothes to the lobby. She expected to find him sleeping, but instead, he seemed to be waiting for her, which made her spirits soar.

~

Finally! Philip had been fighting to keep his eyes open, but now that Katie had arrived, his heart kicked into overdrive, and new energy surged through his body.

And when she handed him his *still-warm-from-the-dryer* pants and shirt, his longing for home and family increased. And he fantasized about who he'd like in the role of wife.

Katie stood before him bashful and demure, but with a hint of that expression she'd worn earlier—teasing and playful. What could he do to bring that part of her to the surface?

Maybe if they had a conversation, he could find out more about her and what made her so hesitant to let her true self show. "Katie, are you too tired to talk?"

Regret flashed in her eyes before she lowered her head. In an apologetic voice, she answered, "A little."

Philip sensed her reluctance, so he didn't push it. Maybe tomorrow they'd be able to be together. It might even be better because they'd both be less tired. Then, Katie dashed that hope.

"I don't want you to think I don't want to spend time with you, but I still have to fold the sheets and get things ready for tomorrow. Plus, I need to be up before six to help prepare breakfast."

She'd only get a few hours of sleep at this point. "I wish I'd known. I wouldn't have kept you up so late. Maybe someone else could have helped me with the birth so you could have gone to bed earlier." Even as he said it, his heart rebelled. He wouldn't have wanted to share that special experience with anyone but Katie.

"It's all right. I enjoyed everything that happened. And seeing the baby born was a miracle." The reverence in her hushed voice made the lobby feel like a cathedral.

Philip agreed. And it definitely was a miracle he'd made no mistakes. With Deshawn and Katie telling him what to do, nothing had gone wrong.

But Katie's answer made it clear she'd be working in the morning and wouldn't have time to talk. He'd have no excuse to hang around here once he woke. Why did that make him so depressed?

He shook himself. Maybe it was for the best. He hadn't planned to stay in the Lancaster area much longer. He'd been drifting from state to state ever since he turned eighteen. Moving around kept him from remembering something he'd rather forget. And it prevented him from forming long-term attachments. He had no desire to be tied down.

So why had one night's encounter left him longing for home and family? And a wife? Had delivering a baby given him a desire to share a connection like Isabella's and Diego's?

Watching the love in their eyes and their tenderness with each other and toward their newborn son had made Philip ache for what they had. If only he could share a bond like that with a special woman. Love might be enough to get him to settle down in one place, to create a permanent home.

But why did the picture that kept coming to mind feature Katie's gentle expressions and soft words?

～

Before he fell asleep, Philip attuned his senses to Katie's. He often did this at the fire station, connecting closely to whoever was staying awake, so he'd know when any calls came in they'd need to respond to. He'd jump up and get ready before the warning blast.

With Katie, the sense that linked him to her remained on high alert, and he stayed in harmony with each of her movements. Every time she turned over, sighed, or *rutsched* in her sleep, he felt it even though she was far across the lobby and hidden in an alcove.

When she jumped out of bed at five thirty, he did too. Groggy-eyed, he followed her to the kitchen, where she stood holding a note and looking frazzled.

Philip headed over. "Is everything all right?"

"*Neh.* Anand left a note. The cook can't make it in this morning, so I need to make breakfast. Usually, I just set out the breakfast dishes and keep the serving dishes filled. I'm not sure how I'll manage that if I'm cooking. And I need to clean the rooms, but I'll have to clean the kitchen before I can start those."

"It's Christmas Day. Can't you skip the rooms for one day?"

She shook her head. "It's my job. Unless people hang a sign on their doorknob saying they don't need their bedding changed, I have to do it."

"Can I do anything to help?"

Katie looked as if she planned to refuse. Philip wasn't about to let her. "You washed my clothes, fixed me a bed, and helped me deliver a baby. It's the least I can do."

A little of last night's humor flashed in her eyes. Was she softening? Philip hoped so.

He added one more plea. "After all, it's Christmas. You can consider it a holiday gift. I'd like to give you a present for all you've done for me."

Her eyes glimmered with tears. "*Ach*, and I have Christmas gifts to give out. When will I have time to do that?"

"Don't cry." Philip reached out and gently brushed away a teardrop trickling down her cheek.

She turned her head away. "You'll think I'm foolish. But I had this dream of inviting everyone to the lobby to hear the Christmas story and giving them each a gift."

"Buying gifts for everyone would be expensive, but maybe you could still do the Christmas story. That wouldn't take long."

"I already have the gifts. They're in the luggage room." Katie picked up a stack of bowls and carried them into the other room, where she set them on a serving counter.

Philip grabbed a nearby stack of plates and followed her. "You bought gifts for everyone?" How could she possibly afford that?

"*Neh*, I only baked cookies."

"For everyone in the hotel?"

Katie headed back into the kitchen to bring out silverware. "I didn't do it all by myself. My seven sisters helped."

"But still . . ." Philip was at a loss for words. Who did that? How many rooms did the inn have? He swallowed hard. Her sweetness and thoughtfulness overwhelmed him.

He picked up napkins and a tiered tray of condiments. "I'll help you."

She looked up at him, eyes shining. "You already are." She pointed to the things he'd helped set out.

"I meant with the presents."

"Just having someone awake with me this early in the morning is a gift."

Her heartfelt declaration touched him. Philip's heart swelled with the thought that he'd brought her a little happiness. But that wasn't all he planned to do for her today.

CHAPTER FIVE

*J*didn't mean to complain. I love my job." Katie bit her lip. "It's just that I'd hoped to do more to make Christmas special for everyone who's so far from home."

But when would she find the time? She could let Philip give out the cookies. But what about the Christmas story? How would she fit it in?

On normal days, she often cleaned rooms until late afternoon. And that's if she started as soon as she arrived. But today with being responsible for breakfast cleanup and having every room full. . .

She didn't like to hurry through her work or do what some girls called "a spit and a polish." Katie didn't think that was right. She didn't just do her work thoroughly to keep her job, although she and *Mamm* needed the money. But making things neat and tidy always lifted her spirits, and she wanted each visitor to have a spotless room.

While Katie worried over the situation, her hands stayed busy setting up the buffet. Philip mirrored her movements, carrying in plastic trays of donuts, bagels, and muffins that she slid into place in the acrylic display cases. As she poured batter into the waffle machine and checked the levels in the juice machine, Philip loaded the cooler with yogurts and filled urns with coffee and hot water.

They moved like well-ordered machines, and Katie barely had to speak to him. He seemed to know instinctively what needed to be done. He topped off cereal dispensers, leaving her free to start cooking bacon, sausage, eggs, and fried potatoes.

"That smells delicious." He leaned closer, sending her pulse scattering in all directions.

When he reached for a crispy piece of potato, she waggled the spatula and pretended to smack at his hand. "*Ach*, no, this is a commercial kitchen. No touching food that will be served to guests. If you're hungry, get a plate, and I'll put some potatoes on it."

He put on a wounded look that made her laugh. "I can wait. Sorry, I didn't know."

"You deserve a special plate for all your help. Seriously, I can dish some of this out now while it's hot and fresh, but you should eat it in the dining area."

"I'd rather be with you."

Katie's heart hopscotched. Did he mean that the way she hoped he did? She often found herself at a loss for words, but this time it was for an entirely different reason. A bubble of hope expanded inside her, so fragile she feared it might burst.

Instead, she concentrated all her attention on loading the metal pan with bacon. "Could you put this in the chafing dish?" she said in a slightly shaky voice. "We have pot holders over there."

"Does it matter which opening?"

Katie shook her head. "Any one is fine." That came out a little steadier.

Once he picked up the deep metal pan and turned his back to exit the kitchen, she let herself stare at him. His broad shoulders, his black bowl-cut hair, his confident stride, so unlike her own.

Nah, he must have been teasing. A man that handsome and sure of himself wouldn't be interested in a mouse like her.

By the time he returned, she'd filled the potato pan. He took it from her and winked.

She held her breath as he turned away. Maybe this was a game for him. Perhaps he flirted with all the girls he met. Or maybe it was more teasing like he'd done earlier. Katie refused to get her hopes up.

Ach, much too late for that. She already had.

As he carried out the sausages, Katie started the scrambled eggs. It was best to do them last so they didn't get too dried out. Although the chafing dish kept them moist, she left extra liquid in them. They'd keep cooking for a while after she placed them in the metal container.

"Last dish," she told him, handing over the eggs.

"That's good, because people are already lined up. I'll go back out and keep an eye on everything. I can let you know if we run out."

We? He acted like they were in this together. Katie's step stayed light as she prepped the next batches of hot food.

Philip stuck his head through the doorway. "Any bread? A few people asked about toast."

"I can't believe I forgot that." She laid out white and wheat bread on two plastic trays. "They go in the display case by the toaster."

He laughed. "I kind of figured that. I should have pointed out it was empty."

"Not your fault." Katie should have remembered. She filled those trays on the mornings she helped in the dining room. She wanted to blame her forgetfulness on a lack of sleep last night, but if she were honest, it might have more to do with the man who just walked out the door. He was proving to be a major distraction.

She mixed up another bowlful of eggs and started cooking more bacon, potatoes, and sausage links. Those containers would soon be empty. She lined up replacement pans in the warmer.

Philip hurried in and out with more pancake batter, refills for muffin and bagel trays, syrup and jelly packets, bread for toast. He topped up the coffee and hot water urns.

Katie kept thanking him with her eyes as she stayed too busy to speak, unless she was directing him to find something.

When the buffet closed, Katie wanted to sink into a chair and snooze. But she had a mountain of dishes to put in the dishwasher. Philip had helped her keep up with some of it by collecting plates as people finished eating.

Breathing out a long, slow breath to ease her tension, Katie took the time for a proper *danke*. "I couldn't have done this without you. You did an amazing job."

"So did you," he shot back. "I can't believe how hard you work."

"This isn't my usual job. We have a cook. I sometimes help out like you did today."

"All I can say is I'm exhausted. I don't know how you do this."

"You're probably tired from lack of sleep."

"That too, but this job runs you off your feet."

And her real job hadn't even started yet. "I need to get the kitchen cleaned up and then do the rooms."

Philip moved her gently away from the sink. "I'll handle the kitchen. You go clean the rooms."

"I can't let you. . ."

Her voice trailed off when he put a finger under her chin and titled her face up so he could look directly into her eyes. Could he hear her heart thumping? Katie struggled to breathe.

"Listen. It's Christmas. This is my gift to you. Now go do your rooms. I invited everyone who came to breakfast to your Christmas party in an hour."

"An hour? I can't do that. I have too much work."

"Don't you get a break? Maybe Anand will let you take your lunch early. Want me to ask him?"

"I can do it." Katie had no trouble talking to Anand. She'd been here long enough that she felt like part of the family.

Most likely with the eight inches of fresh snow that had fallen last night after they'd gone to bed, their visitors would stay in the same rooms. That meant no new rooms to prepare. Perhaps their guests would be flexible on what time their rooms were cleaned. And she wouldn't take long at the Christmas party.

But as Katie pushed the cart of towels and bedding down the hall, each room had a door hanger on it. Every one of them indicated they didn't need towels or bedding changed. This was impossible.

Only one door at the end of the hall had no sign hanging from the doorknob. Katie knocked.

A woman peeked out. "Oh, good. I need four more towels."

Katie handed them to her. "Are you ready for me to clean the room, or should I come back later?"

"No need." The woman reached a hand around and hung a Do Not Disturb sign on the outside of her door. "I'm fine for today. Towels were all I wanted. Merry Christmas."

Katie stood there staring at the door after the woman closed it. She headed for the opposite wing. Two doors didn't have signs. One requested extra shampoo and conditioner. The other asked for towels. As soon as she handed them out, both people insisted they didn't want their rooms cleaned today.

"See you at the Christmas party," one of them said.

"*Jah*, I mean yes." Katie stumbled over her response. She

wasn't sure she should attend. She still had to clean the second floor of each wing.

Dragging her cart into the empty elevator, she pushed the button for the second floor. It seemed strange not to run into people dragging their suitcases out to their cars or rushing to catch flights.

The second floor was a repeat of the first floor. Door hangers hung on almost every doorknob. Again, she handed out towels, body wash, and shampoo. But none of the guests wanted their rooms cleaned.

Katie hustled to put the cart away. Then she got the gifts she and her sisters had wrapped for the three boys and tiptoed to their door. She set them outside and slipped off before the boys could see her.

Forty-five minutes had elapsed. And she was done with her work for the day. She headed to the kitchen.

"That was fast," Philip remarked when she entered. A self-satisfied smile played on his lips.

"Do you know something about this?"

"Who me?" He adopted an innocent injured expression, but Katie could see through his ruse.

She had a sudden, horrible thought. What if he'd played a prank on her? Suppose he'd hung those signs out to tease her?

"Did you—?

"Aww, Katie, don't look so upset. I might have mentioned the signs as I invited them to the Christmas party. I didn't know how many people would cooperate, but I hoped some of them would give you a break."

"Some? How 'bout all of them?"

"All of them?" Philip's eyes widened, but his lips twitched. "That's amazing."

"A few requested towels or toiletries, but that's it. Not one person wanted me to clean the room." *Another miracle.*

"Well, since I finished the dishes, it looks like your Christmas Day is free."

"Oh, you." She punched his arm lightly, playfully. "I can't believe you did that."

His expression grew serious, and his eyes darkened to an even deeper shade of chocolate brown. Like semi-sweet chocolate. Her favorite.

"You deserve a Christmas gift too," he said. "I couldn't make or buy one for you, but I wanted to do something special."

Something special? "This is my best present ever." A spotless kitchen. No rooms to clean. And a Christmas party to attend. She never could have imagined such a wonderful Christmas Day.

CHAPTER SIX

*P*hilip loved Katie's dazed look as she stared around at the immaculate kitchen. And his plan had worked. He'd asked all the guests who'd come to breakfast to give Katie a gift today. He'd never expected everyone in the inn to cooperate. That was awesome.

"Do you need help setting up for the party?" he asked.

"What?"

He'd startled her out of her daydreams. He only wished he could be part of them.

Katie stared off into the distance a moment longer, then she focused on him. "I need to get the cookies from the luggage room. And I'll get a Bible from a hotel room."

Once they had the cookie bags set out under the tree, Katie collected a Bible and marked the passage in Luke. Then she turned to him. "Would you read the Christmas story?"

Philip shook his head. *No way*. With the way he'd rebelled against God, he was the last person to read the Bible. "I can't, Katie. I really can't." He didn't want to confess his past and his failings. She had such a strong faith. She'd never understand his hidden secret or his turning his back on all he'd been taught.

Katie's eyes brimmed with tears. "Please, Philip? I can't speak loudly enough for everyone to hear."

Her soft voice touched a part of him he thought he'd crushed long ago. And he could never turn down anyone who asked for help. But this would be sacrilege. A doubter asking others to listen to the story of Christ's birth?

"Listen, Katie, I would. . ." *I would do anything for you when you look at me with those pleading eyes.* "I would be the wrong person to do this. What about your manager?"

"His voice isn't deep and commanding like yours."

Long eyelashes framing green eyes sparkled with tears. Eyes that reflected God's love. Eyes that begged him to say *jah*. Eyes that touched the depths of his soul.

How could he refuse? "All right."

Her breathless *danke* made his insides whirl with excitement.

People had already started filtering into the lobby. Anand announced over the loud speaker that the Christmas program would begin in five minutes. Doors banged open up and down the halls.

A shriek came from one of the rooms. "Mom, Mom, look! Presents! Santa found us!" a small boy cried out.

Katie stepped over to peek down the hallway, and Philip joined her. One young boy tried to scoop up all the wrapped gifts, while his brothers tried to snatch them.

A tired-looking mother peeked out the door. She appeared flabbergasted. "Where did those come from?" she demanded. "Did you boys steal those from someone?"

"No. I found them outside the door," the oldest boy said.

His mother's eyes narrowed, and she focused on the boxes. "Oh, they do have your names on them. I wonder who did this."

The smallest boy shoved his bigger brothers and snatched at a package. "I want some too."

"Stop fighting." His mom's voice crackled through the air. "Only take the ones with your name on them."

The boys sat in the hallway, ripping off paper and exclaiming over their gifts. From the indulgent expression on Katie's face, she'd been the one who dropped off those presents.

Philip couldn't believe it. Her loving, generous spirit made her a real treasure. The man who had her as his wife would be blessed. Philip wished he could be that man.

He shook himself. What was he thinking? They'd only just met. He'd jumped ahead way too far and much too fast. Besides, what about his plan to keep traveling, to never settle in one place? Marrying meant giving up his dreams. Was he ready to sacrifice his lifelong goals?

Before he could answer his deepest questions, the three boys tore down the hall and headed straight for Katie.

"Look what I got!" The smallest boy zoomed a plastic airplane in circles around her.

She laughed delightedly. A laugh that strummed chords in Philip's soul. A laugh that made him willing to give up all his dreams to create new ones.

Diego assisted Isabella to the lobby and seated her in the comfiest chair, where she sat, cradling the baby. Then, he stood beside them, pride radiating from him. And once again, Philip put himself in Diego's place. More than anything, Philip longed to stand beside a lovely wife and share the joy of a newborn child.

As people gathered, Philip's worry grew. He shouldn't be the one to read this story. He'd made a big mistake in agreeing. Katie's pleading eyes had blinded him to his mistake.

But when she perched on the chair arm beside him, all Philip's excuses fled. And when she leaned in close to whisper in his ear, her breath tickling all his senses, he'd say *jah* to whatever she asked.

"Seeing all the children gave me an idea. Instead of starting with the Bible reading, why don't we sing some Christmas carols first?"

Fine by him. The longer he could put off his part, the better.

"Could you see if anyone would like to volunteer as song leader? Surely, we have at least one guest who's good with music. Unless you'd like to do that too?"

Philip almost agreed, but he caught himself in time. "You want me to ask?"

"Please?"

"I'd be happy to." *And I'd be glad to do anything else you'd like me to do.* But he kept that to himself.

~

When Philip tried to give her his chair, Katie refused, but it filled her with joy.

"I can't," she whispered. "I won't be sitting here long. And it'll be easier for you to read the Bible."

Philip swallowed hard and appeared worried. Did he get as tongue-tied in front of crowds as she did? Katie wished she'd asked him about that, but he seemed so self-assured, and his voice rang with confidence.

Before she could check, Philip cleared his throat and announced they'd start with singing. His voice didn't waver like hers as he asked for a volunteer to lead the music.

A woman raised her hand. "I'm a music teacher. I'd be happy to start everyone off."

She glanced around the room at the crowd seated on chairs, couches, and the floor. Some people had borrowed chairs from the dining area and made several rows behind the couch Philip had slept on last night. One family huddled in the alcove behind the chairs. All seven of them squeezed onto the couch where Katie had spent the night.

Luckily, everyone had left open space in the middle of the floor, so Katie could execute her plan.

The music teacher raised her hand for attention. "Any requests?"

Several people volunteered suggestions. "Away in a Manger." "Silent Night." "We Wish You a Merry Christmas." "Silver Bells."

One of the three brothers called out, "Rudolph the Red-Nosed Reindeer."

Katie had been hoping for more hymns, but with a mixed crowd, she had to accept that not everyone would choose spiritual songs. She nudged Philip, and he glanced up at her expectantly.

"Could you add a few hymns?"

"Of course." He volunteered a few.

Then Diego and Isabella requested "O Little Town of Bethlehem," "Hark, the Herald Angels Sing," and "O Holy Night."

"Well," the music teacher said, "it looks like we have quite a few choices. Why don't we start with 'Rudolph' and save 'Silent Night' for last?

Perfect! Katie wanted that song to end the program. After "Rudolph," the teacher segued into some of the other secular songs. But when she began the hymns, a soft and gentle spirit descended on the room. Even the children who'd been boisterous and restless calmed down.

Sitting beside the towering Christmas tree, its lights softly glowing, and with snow drifting down outside the large picture windows, Katie's heart overflowed. All these strangers had come together to celebrate Christmas. She'd never been away from home and family for the holidays before, yet with Philip's deep bass beside her ear, joining the chorus of voices around the room, she glowed with contentment. In some ways, this felt like a family Christmas because people who'd never met before shared their time with each other.

Several people sat with their eyes closed, tears on their cheeks. Maybe they missed being with their families. Or, Katie hoped, the music had touched their souls and reminded them of the real reason for this holiday season.

Even the children who didn't know all the words to the songs made a joyful noise. Seeing their enthusiasm convinced her the idea she'd had earlier would work.

She bent over to whisper to Philip. If he made the announcement, she'd do all the work.

When she asked, he nodded, and when the song ended, he held up a hand. "Before we sing the next song, Katie would like to meet with all the children in the breakfast room while we sing a few more songs."

Katie flashed him a smile to thank him, and their eyes met and held. A sudden knowing descended over her. Philip was one of the main reasons she felt so at home here today. Something about him called to her. She stood and beckoned to the children to follow her, but she didn't want to leave Philip's presence.

CHAPTER SEVEN

*W*hen Katie left, Philip missed her warmth and her sweet, clear soprano. She didn't say why she'd called the children, but he wished he could join her. Maybe he could slip away during the next Christmas carol. But he changed his mind. If she wanted him, she'd have asked him to accompany her. That made him feel sad and a little left out.

A few songs later, she returned and motioned to Diego. He followed her to the other room and returned in a few minutes to whisper to Isabella who beamed and nodded. Then he left again.

Just before the next song ended, Katie slipped in beside Philip, and her closeness sent tingles throughout his body.

"Can you stop the singing after this song ends? The children would like to present a Nativity play. Could you narrate the story?"

He gulped. He'd been so caught up in the singing, he'd forgotten about the Bible reading.

"As you read, can you pause to let the children act it out?"

Philip nodded. Maybe that would take some of the pressure off him. People would be watching the children. He could pretend to himself that he was the narrator in a play. That would make it easier to ignore the words.

But he'd guessed wrong. When he reached the part about Joseph going to Bethlehem, Diego entered the room wearing a bathrobe over his clothes, and Philip stopped reading.

The oldest of the three brothers, wrapped in a sheet to look like a robe and with a towel draped over his head, stood in front of him and held up a hand. "There's no room in the inn."

Several people tittered. Right now, they were in an inn with no vacancies. But for Philip, it hit with a powerful force. Last night, there'd been no room for this young couple to have their baby. He'd given up his room. And a miracle had happened.

How much more of a miracle was the birth of Christ?

The boy escorted Diego toward Isabella. "Here. You and your wife can stay in the stable."

After Diego thanked him and went to stand beside Isabella, Philip read verse seven, *"And she brought forth her firstborn son, and wrapped him in swaddling clothes, and laid him in a manger; because there was no room for them in the inn."*

He choked back a lump in his throat, remembering baby Jesús wrapped in pillowcases.

As he read the next verses about the shepherds, three young children appeared. They each carried what looked like curtain rods, and they, too, had been draped in sheets. One had a stuffed lamb. There was a small scuffle as they entered.

"It's my lamb," the smallest girl declared and tried to grab it from an older boy.

"But I'm the biggest."

"Give it here." The girl gave the lamb's tail a yank.

Katie's voice came in a hushed whisper. "Let's share like Jesus would want us to."

"Oh, all right. You can have it." The boy thrust it into the little girl's arms,

and she beamed.

An angel came running in, tripped over her robe, and fell on her face. The oldest shepherd helped her to her feet.

She brushed herself off and recited the Bible verses: *"Fear not: for, behold, I bring you good tidings of great joy, which shall be to all people. For unto you is born this day in the city of David a Saviour, which is Christ the Lord."*

The angel pointed the shepherds to baby Jesús as Philip read, *"And this shall be a sign unto you; Ye shall find the babe wrapped in swaddling clothes, lying in a manger."*

Philip paused, letting the words sink in, not just for the audience, but for himself. He'd heard this story so many times, he'd memorized it. The problem with that was he'd never really felt the impact of the words or the story for many years now.

Last night, they'd joked about the baby being wrapped in swaddling clothes, but delivering and holding a newborn had made it all so real. God's Son came to earth as a tiny infant. What a precious gift God had given the world!

The realization choked him up, and he could barely get out the next words. *"And suddenly there was with the angel a multitude of the heavenly host praising God, and saying. . ."*

A group of angels rushed in, flapping their arms. They all spoke together: *"Glory to God in the highest, and on earth peace, good will toward men."*

Philip finished the next few verses to end the story. Though he'd ignored the deeper meaning of the story for years, it struck him today with a powerful force.

He looked up from the Bible. "That wasn't the end of the story. It was only the beginning. That baby had a mission. Jesus had been sent to die for everyone's sins." Then Philip recited John 3: 16.

A soft *Amen* came from Diego. Several others echoed him.

Katie stepped into sight, her eyes shining. *That was perfect*, she mouthed. *Can you read Matthew 2: 1–11?*

Philip fumbled through the pages to find the passage and read of the wisemen and King Herod, who all appeared and said their parts. King Herod exited, but the wisemen bearing gifts bounced up and down as if riding camels.

When they reached the baby, they knelt and set gifts by Isabella's feet—a jar, a bowl, and a wooden box—as Philip ended the reading with *"gold, and frankincense, and myrrh."*

Silence reigned for a minute before the music teacher softly sang the first few words of "Silent Night." Around the room, everyone joined in.

The children formed a beautiful tableau around Isabella as Mary, Diego as Joseph, and baby Jesús as Jesus. The melody soared and swelled in the high-ceilinged room. And Philip's heart expanded with the words when Katie slipped in to sit beside him again.

～

Katie relaxed back, closed her eyes, and let the final stanza of "Silent Night" wash over her. Not everyone knew the words, so they hummed along, and a few guests sang off-key. Yet, the song had never sounded so beautiful to her ears.

Everyone sat in silence after the last notes died away. Some people had tears in their eyes.

When several of them stood, she whispered to Philip. "Can you tell them about the bags under the tree?"

"Before you go," Philip announced, "each of you can take a gift from under the tree made by—"

Katie elbowed him and signaled him with her eyes not to reveal her name.

He reacted quickly. "Made by one of the hotel staff members."

While people picked up their bags or chatted, Katie wove through the crowd to collect the sheets and towels. She'd have piles of extra laundry to do, but she had plenty of time for that because she had no rooms to clean—thanks to Philip.

Philip caught up with her as she carried a load toward the laundry room. She dumped her armful into the washer and turned to find him in the doorway with a huge armload of sheets.

"How did you pull off that program in such a short time?" Admiration shone in his eyes.

Katie couldn't believe how well the spur-of-the-moment Nativity play had gone. The children had cooperated, and she chose the ones who already knew the story and could say the lines, but she had only one answer to his question. "Divine intervention."

His face reddened, and he shifted from foot to foot. "*Jah*, well, you did an incredible job."

"It wasn't me," she insisted. It bothered her that Philip didn't seem to acknowledge God's part in the pageant. That didn't seem to fit with the touching message he'd shared with the crowd.

Philip dumped a load of sheets into the washer next to hers. "You helped. And the kids did great too."

She smiled. "They certainly did." Except for the poor angel who fell on her face and a brief scuffle over the stuffed lamb, everything had gone without a hitch. "I hope it touched people's lives. That's the important thing."

"It touched mine." Philip's voice came out choked. "It's been a long time since I, um, really thought about and appreciated Christ's birth."

Katie stopped adding detergent to the washer and turned toward him. What an odd thing to say. Christ's birth, death, and resurrection were the most important parts of their faith. And Philip had tied them together beautifully with his short speech at the end of the program.

49

Under her scrutiny, his cheeks grew even ruddier. "There's something you should know about me. We need to talk."

"All right. Let me get the rest of the sheets in the washer first."

"I'll help."

Together they gathered Diego's bathrobe and the remaining costumes. Katie loaded them into the washers. Once they were running, she headed for the quiet alcove where she'd slept. People still milled around the lobby, chatting and enjoying their cookies. But the niche gave them some privacy.

Last night, Katie had been discouraged about not having someone to pair off with at the youth group caroling. Today, she'd not only caroled with a large group of people, but she also might be starting a relationship, if the looks Philip had been giving her last night and this morning were any indication.

But he sank onto the far end of the couch, as if he were deliberately staying as far away as possible. Katie couldn't help being disappointed. She'd been hoping. . .

His first words proved encouraging. "Katie, I have to be honest. I've been falling for you."

Her spirits soared as they had during the Christmas carols. At long last, she'd found the man for her. She'd been admiring him since she met him, and her appreciation had only grown in the time they'd spent together. Although she hadn't known him long, she'd been drawn to him.

Before she could admit her feelings, Philip dashed all her hopes with one word. "But. . ."

CHAPTER EIGHT

*W*ith Katie's shining eyes on him, Philip couldn't bring himself to say what he needed to say. Everything about her called to him. Her quiet demeanor calmed his racing mind, his tense muscles, his fidgety body. If anyone was the complete opposite of him, it had to be this girl with her gentle manner, her whispery voice, and her big heart.

And they were complete opposites in one other area—the area that would break their connection if he told the truth. But Katie was too special, too precious. He couldn't lie to her.

The glow in her eyes had faded when he said *but*, so she must care about him too. At least a little. He hated hurting her, but she needed to know the truth.

He swallowed down his regrets. "Katie, there's something you need to know about me."

The disappointment on her face changed to concern and caring. What an incredible person she was. She'd push aside her needs to help others. He couldn't believe what he was giving up. But he cared too much about her to lead her on.

"I admire your faith, and I wish mine matched yours." But it didn't, and it never would. He had a huge gaping hole in his heart where God should be.

Katie tilted her head to one side as if trying to understand. "Faith isn't something to be measured against another person's. And what you see on the outside of people doesn't always reflect what's in their hearts."

"Exactly. That's what I'm trying to explain. I look Amish on the outside, but I'm not in my heart."

"You're not with the church?"

How could he explain the complicated mess of his life? "I was baptized at seventeen, but then something happened, and I lost my faith."

Concern drew her brows together, but her eyes reflected puzzlement.

"Well, not my faith exactly. I still believe in God, but I don't want to be part of the church."

"I don't understand. You don't go to church? You've been shunned?"

He shook his head. "I attend services out of habit. Not because I want to be there."

Katie stayed silent, as if encouraging him to continue. He studied her face but saw no sign of judgment or condemnation. She seemed to sincerely want to understand. If everyone in the church had been as kind as her, Philip might not have run from attachments and from the faith.

"In my heart, I've left the Amish community and the faith. I may go to church on Sundays, but I'm dead inside."

"*Ach*, Philip."

Those two soft words touched the wounded part of him. He wanted to tell her the whole story.

"When I was eighteen, about a year after I joined the church, my younger sister, um. . ." Philip's face heated. Men didn't talk about these things with women. Yet, he wanted Katie to know.

"I see." Katie didn't look at him when she said it, but he could tell she understood.

"Beth had just joined the church, but she wasn't dating anyone. She refused to name the father. She just crawled into her shell and refused to speak."

Philp relived that time in his mind. Tongues clucked, and everyone looked at her askance. "You know how fast gossip spreads in the Amish community."

Katie nodded, and her sympathetic expression encouraged him to continue.

"She was shunned, of course, but when my parents and the bishop talked to her about marrying the father, she ran from the room, and . . . and took off in the buggy."

Clenching his fists at his side, he struggled to finish. "She was driving recklessly. She missed the stop sign at the intersection. A car clipped her, and she was thrown from the buggy."

Katie sucked in a breath.

"She only lived a few days, but she lived long enough to tell me the baby's father." He squeezed his eyes shut. Even now, five years later, he could still feel Beth's grip on his fingers and see the terror on her face as she struggled to form the name. Once she'd said it, her eyes closed, and her hand went slack.

"A deacon at our church. A married man. He'd threatened her."

Katie reached out, and her hand closed over his. The warmth of her fingers erased the old memories. Gratitude welled in Philip's heart.

"After the funeral, I confronted him. He denied it. Deep inside, I was convinced Beth had told the truth. But what could I do? I thought about going to the bishop, but I had no proof."

Philip groaned and hung his head. The gentle pressure of Katie's hand kept him grounded.

"I wish I had. I blame myself for what happened next. Six months later, another girl. . ."

Katie gasped.

"That girl didn't keep quiet. The deacon confessed, and everyone forgave him. I went to him afterwards and asked why he didn't mention Beth in his confession, and he called my sister a liar."

"I'm so sorry." Katie's gentle voice soothed Philip's spirit.

But it couldn't defuse the rage bubbling inside. "Later, I found out the bishop knew the deacon had preyed on several girls. The bishop spoke to the deacon and accepted his promise to stop."

Philip longed to pound something. "Those hypocrites."

"I can understand why you're upset. It's horrible to lose your sister that way. And it doesn't seem fair for her to suffer for someone else's wrongs."

"Exactly." Philip's throat tightened. He'd never told anyone this story. Not even his parents. All the old poison seemed to be draining out until only fury remained.

"I couldn't forgive that man. And I couldn't stay in that church. I went to stay with an *onkel* in a different community, but that wasn't far enough away. I've been on the road ever since, staying three or four months before moving on. I'm too restless to stay in one place."

"Are you really restless? Or just running from the truth?"

Katie's question stopped him dead. "What do you mean?"

"I'm not trying to judge you, Philip, but have you forgiven the deacon?"

"*Neh.* I can't. He's a hypocrite, and so is the bishop. They're supposed to be leaders we can look to as examples. And what about the community with their gossip? Every church I go to is the same. If more people lived like you. . ."

"I hope nobody ever looks to me as an example. They'll find I don't always live the way I should. I'd cause others to stumble."

Philip doubted that. She'd never cause anyone to stumble.

Well, except maybe stumble into love with her. Those gorgeous green eyes, so open, so caring, flipped his stomach upside down and inside out.

"Besides," Katie continued, "we're not supposed to look at other people to show us how to live. We have Jesus. He should be our only example."

If Katie had been his example, Philip doubted he'd ever have left the church. But that was wrong. As she'd reminded him, he shouldn't use other people as a standard. Still, how did he handle the hypocrisy—the cruelty—he'd seen?

"What about my sister? People who claimed to follow God destroyed her life."

"I'm so sorry for your pain, Philip, and sorry your sister lost her life. You've had to deal with some terrible things. But there's only one answer. Forgiveness."

Katie's simple response echoed years of church teachings. Teachings Philip struggled to put into practice. He found it easier to forgive people who did him wrong than to pardon those who caused his sister's suffering.

"I can't."

"I can only imagine how hard it would be. If I lost one of my sisters. . ." Katie bit her lip. "It's heartbreaking. I know we're told to forgive others so God can forgive us. But forgiving also rids us of the poison inside that's hurting us."

Poison. Philip had used that word many times to describe the anguish that festered inside him each time he thought of the past. He'd been running for a long time now, but he'd never gotten away. He'd carried it with him to every new place, to every church, to every community. And it had affected his relationships, his spirituality, his whole life.

Another gentle squeeze to his hand caused his heart to swell with love. If only he could get to the point of forgiveness, he'd have more love to give. But that shouldn't be his motivation. He should do it because of obedience to God.

"When I struggle to do something I should," Katie said softly, "I pray and ask the Lord to make me willing."

She seemed so in tune with his struggles. Had she read his mind?

"Would you like me to pray with you?" she asked.

The tenderness in her voice pierced a hole in his resistance. Overcome by her caring, he choked up and could only nod.

Beside him, Katie bowed her head. "Dear Lord, You know how hard this is for Philip. Please give him the willingness to turn everything over to You."

A warmth burned inside Philip, filling him with a desire to surrender, to stop fighting God's will. With sudden clarity, he realized he could never forgive others until he accepted God's forgiveness for his own sins.

His throat too tight to let words pass, he begged silently, *Father, please forgive me.* Years of burdens rolled from his heart. *And please give me the grace and strength to forgive all of those I've held a grudge against*—he sucked a painful breath into his constricted lungs—*including the bishop and— and. . . the deacon.*

A small ray of God's light shone into his soul. Gradually, it expanded until it filled him, both searing and cleansing him. Freeing him—at last.

When he lifted his head, his eyes met Katie's, and without a word, she made it clear she understood. He pressed her hand, relishing their silent connection.

Philip had a sudden vision of them praying together in the future as husband and wife. More than anything he longed for that.

He'd intended to explain to Katie why he was wrong for her. But now no obstacle stood in their way. Except. . . his fear of asking her. What if she said *neh*? How would he bear it?

"Philip," she said in a soft, gentle voice filled with under-standing. "You can ask me."

"How did you know?"

She smiled. "I have my ways."

"Could you tell I made things right with God?"

"The glow in your eyes told me that. Before their depths were sad and shuttered. Now they're open and clear."

Amazing. As amazing as she was. "*Jah*, I needed to ask the Lord for forgiveness first. Otherwise, I could never have forgiven anyone else."

Her sweet smile touched places deep within him. She'd already issued an invitation to ask her, so he gathered his courage. Taking a deep breath, he asked his second most important question of the day. "Katie, may I court you?"

And he got the answer he was longing to hear—the softest, sweetest *jah*. Another Christmas miracle.

A CHRISTMAS TO TREASURE

CHAPTER ONE

*W*ould you like to get married?"

The heady scent of coffee brewing nearly gagged Rose Beiler. How could her best friend be so cruel? They'd just finished pieces of chocolate cake at their favorite bakery, Rebecca's Porch, to celebrate Rose's thirtieth birthday.

Blinking back tears, Rose said in a choked voice, "If it's God's will."

Suzanne leaned forward, and her intensity shook the rickety wooden table covered with a pink floral tablecloth. "Did you ever think God allowed you to stay single this long for a purpose?"

"I'm sure He did." Although for the life of her, Rose had no idea why, unless He intended for her to take care of her parents when they aged. If so, she'd be single for a long time. Maybe forever.

"Would you marry a widower with children?" Suzanne's eyes bored into Rose.

At this point, Rose wouldn't care if he had twenty children, but she didn't want Suzanne to sense her desperation. "If that's what God wants for me."

Suzanne studied Rose with an intensity that made her uncomfortable. "You like children, right?"

Rose almost snapped at her. *I've babysat your two often enough.* But she loved her friend too much to be mean. "Of course I do. I often babysit."

Rose volunteered to watch the children of other *mamms* her age from their buddy bunch at church. And she watched her nieces and nephews as often as she could.

"I know you do." Suzanne softened a little. "I meant as in having a widower's children all the time."

"I've never thought about it." The two older widowers at church had teenagers. Neither of those men appealed to Rose.

"Think about it now and tell me."

Rose tried hard not to screw up her face. "Are you trying to match me up with Simon or Paul?"

Suzanne burst out laughing. "No wonder you scrunched up your face. No, silly, I have a different, much younger widower in mind."

A relieved breath escaped Rose, but then she tensed. What other widowers did Suzanne know? Maybe someone at the GreenValley Farmer's Market where she worked? "Who?" Rose asked cautiously.

"My brother."

"Joshua?" Even saying his name brought her teenage crush back full force.

"Ever since his wife died, her sister's been watching the children, but she's sick. Joshua sold his house in New York and plans to move back to Lancaster to take over *Daed's* construction business. He'll need someone to help with the children."

"I'd be happy to help any time." *More than happy.* She'd do anything for Joshua King.

Suzanne laughed. "I think he'll need more than a part-time babysitter. The two oldest girls will be in school, but the little ones are four-years-old and fifteen months. I thought you'd make the perfect wife."

Rose's heart fluttered. "He wouldn't be interested in me."

"Joshua liked you when we were younger."

"He did?"

"Don't you remember how he used to stare at you when we were together?"

"He was looking at me?" She'd always thought he was keeping an eye on Suzanne.

"Of course." Suzanne's brisk answer seemed to be an attempt to brush away Rose's doubts.

Marry Joshua King? Her childhood dream come true? What else could Rose say but *jah*?

~

Joshua leaned back in his chair at the supper table. "It's so good to be home."

"We're glad to have you here." *Mamm* stood and gathered plates. "We missed you so much while you were in New York."

Ten years ago, Joshua and Lena had purchased a farm in Fort Plain, so they hadn't been able to visit very often. He'd missed Lancaster and his family.

Daed sighed. "If we'd known you were coming back, we wouldn't have made plans to move to Lititz."

In the last letter *Mamm* had sent to Fort Plain, she'd mentioned Joshua's older brother was building a *dawdi haus* attached to his farmhouse.

"When will the house be finished?" Joshua asked.

"It already is," *Daed* said. "Merv hoped you and I would help him finish a few interior details this weekend. We were planning to move in next—" He stopped abruptly when *Mamm* frowned and darted a look at Joshua.

"We'll stay here as long as you need us," she reassured him.

Daed leaned forward. "So, *sohn*, do you have any plans for, um, how you'll take care of the girls while you work?"

"I can take care of them," Joshua's ten-year-old daughter, Hannah, announced.

"I'm sure you do a fine job." *Mamm* picked another stack of plates and flashed a *let's-drop-this* look in *Daed*'s direction.

He ignored her signal. "But he'll need someone while Hannah is in school."

Mamm swished into the kitchen. "Let's give Joshua some time to get settled."

A loud thump on the front door interrupted them.

"That'll be Suzanne. She's dropping off our meat order," *Mamm* called over the running water. "Joshua, can you help your sister bring in the boxes?"

He hurried to the door and carried the first box of chicken parts into the kitchen. Then he helped Suzanne unload several more batches.

"Not those," she said as he reached for the two remaining boxes. "The rest is mine. I can't believe how much *Mamm* ordered this time, but I guess she does have five more people to feed."

Was his sister trying to make him feel guilty? If so, she'd done a great job.

"Thanks, Suzanne." *Mamm* shooed her out of the kitchen after they'd set down the last boxes. "I know you want to spend some time with Joshua." She called to Hannah, "Why don't you and Lillian do the dishes while I take care of the meat?"

"*Daed*," Suzanne said, "I'm sure Emily and Faith would love to have you read them a bedtime story."

"Good idea." His *daed* picked up the baby, and four-year-old Emily took his hand.

What was going on? His sister seemed to be clearing the room. Were his parents in on this?

Suzanne sat across the dining room table from him. "Did

you know *Mamm* and *Daed* planned to move into the *dawdi haus* next weekend?"

"That soon?"

Mamm had interrupted *Daed* before he'd given their moving date.

"Well, now they won't. Not until you have someone to care for the children. Have you thought about what you're going to do?"

"I don't know." Joshua felt like he'd been smacked with a steel beam. He'd assumed *Mamm* would be around for a while. Now he'd have to figure that out. He already had enough on his mind with taking over *Daed*'s construction business. He'd expected *Daed* to stick around to help with that, too.

"Have you thought about getting married?"

What? Joshua sat bolt upright.

A dish slammed down in the kitchen, and Hannah burst through the doorway. "I don't want a new *mamm*."

"Hush, Hannah." But, to tell the truth, Joshua didn't either.

Hannah pouted. "If you marry someone, she'll never be our *mamm*. Right, Lillian?"

His nine-year-old daughter peeked out from behind Hannah and nodded. She usually followed her older sister's lead.

Don't worry, girls. I won't be adding a mamm *to our family.* Besides, Suzanne shouldn't even be talking about this. Dating, which he had no intention of doing, should be his decision. And it should be private.

His sister chatted about other things until *Mamm* had taken the girls up to bed. Then Suzanne cornered Joshua before he headed upstairs.

"I know the perfect wife for you. She loves children, and she's always liked you."

"I'm not interested."

"You haven't even heard who it is."

He tried to walk around her, but she blocked the stairway. It didn't matter who she had in mind. He had no plans to marry.

"Rose Beiler."

"She's not married?" That surprised him. She'd been sweet, kind, and pretty. He could tell she'd been attracted to him when they were teens. He'd been interested in her as well, but she was six years younger. He couldn't believe she'd never married.

"You broke her heart when you married and moved away."

"Don't be ridiculous." Even if Rose had cared for him long ago, she wouldn't have waited for him all this time.

"Rose is willing to marry you."

"You asked her?" Joshua couldn't believe his sister had done that. "I can't afford to marry." Even selling his home to move here had made only a little dent in the amount he owed for Lena's cancer treatments.

"You can't afford not to. You work long hours. How much will it cost to hire someone to take care of the children?"

"I don't know, but—"

Suzanne didn't let him finish. "The only cost in marrying is adding one more person to the meals."

Neh, it had emotional costs as well. Costs Joshua wasn't ready to pay.

When he set his lips and didn't answer, she rambled on. "A wife can save you at least that much money. She can make economical meals, grow vegetables in the garden and can them, mend the clothes, do household chores, and free you to spend more time at work."

Joshua held up a hand to stop her. "I'm not ready to remarry." And he doubted he ever would be.

"This isn't about you. What about your children? *Mamm* and *Daed*?"

Could he marry for his daughters' sakes? His parents' sakes? Was that fair to Rose?

Taking his silence for agreement, Suzanne stood. "I'll tell Rose you're interested."

"Wait, I didn't say—"

Without letting him finish his sentence, his sister rushed out the door and shut it behind her.

Now what?

CHAPTER TWO

*R*ose headed to the Green Valley Farmer's Market to get dried apples for *schnitz* pie. Church would be at their house that Sunday.

First, she stopped at Suzanne's craft stand. Fall-themed quilts hung on the wall. Dried cornstalks and pumpkins decorated each end of the booth. Crafts from the local Amish communities crowded all the surfaces. Faceless dolls, grapevine wreaths, wooden toys, baskets, and birdhouses dotted the spaces between quilts and pillows.

Suzanne leaned close and whispered, "I talked to Joshua last night. You'll have to be patient with him because he's still grieving Lena. But he did light up when I mentioned you. I told him I'd let you know he's interested."

"*Ach,* Suzanne, really?"

After her friend nodded, Rose floated on air as she headed to buy the dried apples. Joshua wanted to marry her? She'd not only get to be a wife and mother, but she'd get to be with the man of her dreams.

When she arrived home with the *schnitz, Mamm* stopped

scrubbing the baseboards and stared. "My goodness, you look cheerful."

"It's a lovely day." Rose fought to compose her expression into a neutral smile, but her lips kept curving into a broad grin.

Mamm's eyebrows rose. "Really?" She twisted around to stare out at the dreary gray sky. "The wind chilled my hands when I hung out the wash."

Rose could have sworn the sun had been shining. Or maybe all the warmth and sunshine radiated from her heart.

Her *mamm* faced her again. "What's going on, *dochder*?"

Although Rose should keep her news secret until Joshua spoke with her, she couldn't resist sharing.

Rocking back on her heels, *Mamm* studied Rose. "I know you've always cared for Joshua, but will you be content being a mother to his children if he hasn't gotten over his wife?"

Mamm's words popped Rose's bubble of joy.

"That won't be easy." Not having his heart might be the most painful thing she'd have to face. But Rose had enough love for both of them.

"*Neh*, it won't," *Mamm* agreed. "But the children do need a mother, and maybe in time . . ."

Rose vowed to give Joshua whatever time he needed to heal.

Her mother dropped the cloth in the bucket, wiped her hands on her apron, and embraced Rose. "God has a purpose in all this, I'm sure."

Rose had no doubt of that. All those years ago, she'd prayed for Joshua to wait for her. And now . . .

Could her spirit soar any higher?

～

Joshua yawned. He'd finally gotten all four girls to sleep, so he headed downstairs for a bedtime snack. He had to get up early to help *Daed* finish a house for an *Englisch* customer.

As he walked through the living room, the front door snicked open, and Suzanne waltzed in, her face wreathed in smiles.

Rather than returning his sister's enthusiastic greeting, Joshua struggled to smile. Something deep inside sent up warning flares.

"Rose said *jah*! She's thrilled."

Mamm peeked out of the kitchen. "*Jah* to what, Suzanne?" But his *mamm*'s glowing eyes indicated she already knew the answer.

"I already told you—" Joshua tried not to growl.

"If only you'd seen her face. She glowed."

A picture of Rose's shining face flashed through Joshua's mind. When they were younger, she always lit up whenever he spoke to her. She'd been so pretty, so excited, so young. Fourteen to his twenty. A huge age difference. Now, though, the gap wouldn't seem so large.

"I was right. You do like her. I can tell by your expression."

"How could I? I haven't seen her in years."

"She's such a sweet girl." *Mamm* pinned Joshua with a pointed look.

Was the entire family in on Suzanne's scheme? Despite his sister's plotting, Joshua was certain about one thing. He couldn't take on a wife for many reasons. As much as he disliked hurting Rose's feelings, he needed to find out what his sister had told Rose and clear up any misunderstandings.

～

All day Saturday, Rose and her sisters baked two dozen *schnitz* pies and scoured the kitchen. For the past week, Rose's *aentis*, sisters, sisters-in-law, and cousins had been helping *Mamm* scrub every room. Rose helped whenever she had time off work. Now she had even more incentive to make everything perfect for holding church at their house tomorrow.

She fell into bed exhausted on Saturday night and struggled to sleep. In a few more hours, she'd see Joshua for the first time since he'd returned to Lancaster. And, as the butterflies flitting inside her stomach kept reminding her, he wanted to marry her.

She woke early on Sunday morning after a fitful sleep and took special care with her appearance. She'd barely finished washing the breakfast dishes when Suzanne burst into the kitchen carrying a little girl. Three more girls trailed behind Suzanne's two daughters.

"I thought you should get to know Joshua's girls, so we came early. He'll be here later with *Mamm* and *Daed*."

Suzanne introduced each girl, and Rose's heart expanded in her chest as Suzanne handed over Faith. The small girl snuggled close to Rose and closed her eyes. A few curls had escaped from Faith's tiny braids, reminding Rose of Joshua's light brown hair. She couldn't believe she was holding his daughter.

Later, as they filed into church, *Mamm* smiled to see Rose holding the sleeping little one. Suzanne seated Emily next to Rose, and Suzanne's daughters sat on either side of her. The two older girls sat beside Joshua's *mamm*. Rose would have liked to get to know them as well, but she'd do that after church.

Suzanne had brought a few small toys and snacks, which she passed out. Emily selected a miniature wooden horse and galloped it over Rose's leg. Rose smiled down at Emily, and the little girl smiled back. What a privilege it would be to mother these precious girls.

~

Joshua's stomach still roiled as the men filed into the church from the barn. He regretted arguing with Suzanne this morning when she came to pick up his daughters.

He'd been in the middle of telling Suzanne he'd never marry anyone when Hannah entered the kitchen. Joshua had stopped mid-sentence and glared at his sister. He didn't feel right sitting in church without asking for her forgiveness.

He also needed to explain the truth to Rose. He had no idea how he'd do that.

Joshua's gaze strayed past his sister and her two daughters to Emily and—and Rose. His chest tightened at her tenderness with Faith. And when she smiled down at his small daughter, it took his breath away.

Rose lifted her head and met his stare. Her cheeks flushed, and her lips parted as they curved upward. Suddenly shy, she lowered her head, but not before he glimpsed her dewy-eyed look. If anyone had seen that, they'd get the wrong idea.

Joshua struggled to keep his mind on the sermons, but he spent more time checking out Rose. His sister had been right. Rose would be the perfect *mamm* for his motherless girls. Except . . . he couldn't consider taking a wife.

～

As the women headed for the kitchen after the service, Hannah sidled over to Rose and snarled in a low voice, "My *daed* doesn't want to marry you."

Suzanne shushed Hannah. "That's not true."

Hannah thrust out her lower lip. She wilted a little under Suzanne's stern glare, but muttered, "He doesn't."

Rose's happiness shriveled under the fierceness of Hannah's fury.

Suzanne sidled closer to Rose and kept her voice low. "Ignore her. She's just upset at the thought of her *daed*—"

"What are you two whispering about?" Hannah studied Suzanne suspiciously. Then she turned to Rose. "*Daed* doesn't need your help. He has me."

See? Suzanne mouthed. *She's jealous.* She patted Hannah on the shoulder. "Your *daed* will still need you."

But Hannah had planted doubts in Rose's mind. Did Joshua really want to marry her?

The thought nagged at her during the meal, but as everyone began to leave, Joshua rapped at the kitchen door. Joy filled her. Hannah had been wrong.

"Rose, could I talk to you? Maybe later today?"

Her pulse thumped out an excited rhythm, but she tried to act calm. "Any time is fine." The sooner, the better. She couldn't wait.

"I'll stop by as soon as the two youngest ones are down for their naps." Then, without looking directly at her, he hurried off.

Rose tried not to mind his abrupt departure. He had four daughters to care for, and she'd need to share him. Besides, he'd be coming alone this afternoon. At least, she hoped that's what he'd planned. She'd have him all to herself.

～

Joshua sighed. Going to talk to Rose in the kitchen had been a mistake. Many of the women shot knowing smiles his way. He'd started exactly the kind of gossip he'd been hoping to avoid. And Rose's excitement and starry eyes didn't bode well for what he had to tell her.

Even his parents exchanged knowing looks as he climbed into the buggy with Faith and Emily. Hannah and Lillian had begged to ride with their cousins.

"Faith really took to Rose, didn't she?" *Mamm* said as she settled into the front seat.

Jah, she had. And so had Emily. Maybe he could ask Rose about babysitting them. Or maybe not. That might start even more rumors.

When they reached the house, *Mamm* offered to put the two younger girls down for their naps. Joshua had no excuse to put off his talk with Rose.

Suzanne and her husband pulled into the driveway as Joshua hitched up the team. His sister hopped from the buggy to let Hannah and Lillian out.

With a self-satisfied smile, Suzanne headed in his direction. Joshua wished he'd already left.

"Going to see Rose?"

He ignored his sister's question and climbed into the buggy.

Suzanne's teasing voice floated after him. "You'd better come back here engaged. Rose is fine with skipping the usual dating. She'll understand if you want to marry right away."

Steaming, Joshua headed for Rose's house. Partway there, he slowed. If he showed up so soon after he'd left, Rose and her parents might mistake it for eagerness to spend time with her. He turned in the opposite direction at the next crossroad and drove around for a while, but that only increased his nervousness.

After enough time had passed, he headed to her house, where he found the family gathered around the kitchen table. Rose's *mamm* made a show of catching her *daed*'s eye and leaving Joshua and Rose alone.

Gut. Having Rose across the table and her parents in the other room discouraged any thoughts of romance.

Joshua plunged into what he'd come to say. "I know my sister talked to you. But I want to make things clear. About dating, I, um"—he swallowed hard—"well, I don't want to. It's not—"

"It's all right." Rose's voice was sweet and soothing.

He exhaled a long, relieved sigh. "I'm so glad you

understand."

"*Jah*, I do. Suzanne explained how difficult it is for you to go anywhere when you have four children, so I'm fine without dating. I could come to the house and make meals or do something with the children." She stopped speaking when he frowned.

"I didn't mean for you to come to the house."

"I don't mind. I'm happy to watch the girls and make meals. It'll be the easiest way for the children to get used to me."

They seemed to be talking at cross-purposes. He had to make this clearer. "It's only been a year since Lena passed, so I'm not really ready for—"

Rose squeezed her eyes shut. "I don't know what it's like to lose someone you loved so deeply, but I'm sure healing takes time."

"You don't understand."

"I know I don't, but I'm willing to mother the girls and take care of the house. I know I can never take"—she lowered her head and sucked in a breath—"Lena's place."

She'd accept that? They didn't have to have a relationship? Joshua couldn't believe she'd said that. "But it's not fair to you. You deserve someone who can love you with a whole heart."

"So far, that hasn't happened." Rose sounded as if she were holding back tears. "As Suzanne pointed out, maybe God has kept me single all this time for this very reason."

He set his hands on the table and leaned forward to explain that God hadn't been planning for her to be his wife. Then it struck him. He hadn't prayed before he came here. How could he be so certain of God's will?

Instead, he asked, "You've prayed about this?"

Her eyes shone with certainty. "I feel like God is leading me to do this."

She reached across the table to lay a gentle hand on his clenched fist, and her touch ignited a spark he quickly tamped down. But he barely heard her next words as long-buried feelings for her bubbled to the surface.

Rose's expression filled with sympathy. "I can tell you feel guilty, but it's all right. I, well, you may wonder what I'd get out of the marriage." Her cheeks turned a pretty shade of pink.

Joshua couldn't understand why other men had passed her by. She had a beauty, an earnestness, an honesty. *Wait a minute. Don't go falling for her.*

"It's been painful to be single and watch my other friends marry and have children. I wondered if God would ever give me a home and family of my own."

Her downcast eyes spoke of her shame, her hurt at being rejected. How could he reject her too?

"When Suzanne told me about you," Rose continued, "I thanked God that He'd given me this chance. I know you're still missing, still tied to"—she hesitated before saying his wife's name—"Lena. But I'll do my best to take care of your children and the home."

He'd come to tell her he couldn't marry her. Instead, somehow, he'd dug himself in deeper. If he told her he'd never want to marry, that he didn't plan to marry her, he'd crush her. He couldn't bring himself to dash the joy on her face.

~

After Joshua left, Rose's hopes shriveled. He didn't love her. She'd always hold second place to Lena. Could she go through with this? If she had enough love for both of them, maybe in time . . .

Still, her heart ached. She'd always longed to be in love, but in her dreams, the man loved her back. Instead, she'd be heading into a loveless marriage.

Although God seemed to be leading her to accept this situation, another part of her cried. But Joshua and the children needed her. How could she put her romantic fantasy above their needs?

She'd also be giving up her dream of a big wedding. A second marriage was always shorter and smaller, so they'd only have immediate family and a few friends.

Not long after Joshua left, Suzanne knocked on the door. Had she been spying on her brother?

"I came to help you get ready for the singing," Suzanne said.

"Really?" Sarcasm leaked into Rose's question. Her friend had never helped before when they had the youth over.

"*Ach*, Rose, don't tease. What did he say?"

"He doesn't really want to get married." Although Joshua didn't use those words, that's the message Rose read in his expression. If she hadn't prattled on, she feared he might have said exactly that.

Suzanne's face fell. "You two are perfect for each other."

Rose agreed. Or they would be, if Joshua loved her.

"Listen," Suzanne said, before the teens began arriving, "I also came to ask if you could make supper for Joshua and the girls tomorrow night. *Mamm* and *Daed* have plans to meet some friends at Yoder's."

"Of course. I'll make something and drop it off after work."

"Not drop it off. Eat with them so the girls can get to know you. Plus, it'll let Joshua see what a great cook you are."

"Suzanne, are you sure Joshua wants to do this?" Rose didn't only mean the meal. She also meant the marriage.

"I'm certain he does. Could you be there when Hannah and Lillian get home from school? *Mamm* could use a break."

The first teens had driven their buggies into the driveway, so Rose only nodded. By the time she realized Suzanne had off from the market on Mondays and could watch the girls and make the meal, her friend had slipped out the door.

Rose sighed. What if Suzanne was pushing too hard? What if Joshua really *didn't* want to marry her?

CHAPTER THREE

*W*hen Rose arrived at the Kings' house on Monday, Joshua's *mamm* met her at the door and helped her carry in the pasta, a jar of homemade spaghetti sauce, salad ingredients, and lemon bars for dessert.

"Joshua will love this meal. Lemon bars are his favorite."

Rose remembered that from when he attended singings. "I hope he likes spaghetti."

"It's also one of his favorites, along with chicken pot pie, so you've made a *gut* choice."

Chicken pot pie. Rose tucked that into her memory for the next time she made him a meal. If she did.

"*Danke* for doing this." Joshua's *mamm* hugged Rose. "The two little ones will wake from their naps soon, and the older girls should be home shortly. Suzanne wanted me to run by and help her with some sewing before we go to the restaurant, so I'll leave everything to you."

Sewing? Since when did Suzanne need help with that? She'd been making crafts and quilts for years.

When Rose was alone, she tiptoed upstairs to check on the

sleeping children. She smoothed wisps of hair from their faces, and her heart swelled. Would these be her daughters?

A door banged open downstairs. "We're home," Hannah shouted.

The noise woke Emily, who whimpered and sat up.

Rose lowered herself onto the bed and wrapped an arm around the small girl. "Would you like a snack?"

Bleary-eyed, Emily stared at Rose, a small frown puckering her forehead. "Where's *Mammi*?"

"She's helping Suzanne. Will you come with me?"

Emily nodded and took Rose's hand.

Hannah hollered up the stairs. "*Mammi*, where are you?" When Rose appeared at the top of the stairs with Emily, Hannah's chin jutted out. "What are you doing here?"

"Making supper for all of you."

"Not for me, you're not. I can make supper for my *daed*."

"*Gut*." Rose headed into the kitchen. "I'd be glad for the help."

Lillian came into the kitchen. "Hannah left her scooter in the driveway."

"Tattletale." Hannah glared at her sister until Lillian shrank back.

Rose kept her voice gentle. "I'm sure you don't want it to be in your *daed*'s way when he drives the team up the driveway."

Hannah turned narrowed eyes in Rose's direction, but then she stomped outside. When she returned, Emily had perched on a chair beside Rose to help wash lettuce. Lillian was digging in the cupboard for the pots.

"Is this one big enough?" Lillian held up a large soup pot.

Hannah snatched the pot from her. "I know how to cook spaghetti."

"We should wait until it's almost time for your *daed* to get home to cook the pasta," Rose suggested. "But you could heat the water."

"You do it," Hannah ordered Lillian, handing her the pot and watching with a mutinous expression on her face as her sister filled and lifted the heavy pot.

"Hannah, could you heat up the sauce?" Rose asked.

Hannah flung open the cupboard door and clattered the pots before she retrieved one. After she opened the sauce, she turned up her nose. "This smells like it's bad."

Rose took the jar and sniffed. "I think it'll be fine."

With a huff, Hannah dumped it into the pot, splattering sauce on the counter and stovetop. Rose decided against asking her to clean up and wiped the spills herself.

As Joshua pulled into the driveway, Faith whined from her crib upstairs.

"Can you put the spaghetti into the pot now?" Rose asked Lillian.

Hannah marched over. "I'll do it."

Rose hurried upstairs to change Faith's diapers. From the window, Rose stared at Joshua while he unhitched the horse and pulled the buggy into the barn. As a teenager, she'd stood here in Suzanne's room sometimes to watch him. Only now his shoulders had broadened, and he had a beard.

The beard reminded Rose he'd belonged to another woman. A sharp, swift pang shot through her.

She refused to let herself dwell on that. Joshua would finish rubbing down the horse soon and come inside to eat. Rose wanted to be sure everything was ready. With Faith in her arms, she hurried downstairs.

The spaghetti boiled in the pot, and Hannah was stirring the simmering sauce. Lillian was sopping up a spill that smelled like vinegar. Beside her, a container of pepper had tipped over. Rose closed it and put it back on the spice rack.

"*Danke*, girls. It looks like you can make meals on your own."

The door opened, and Joshua stopped and stared. "Rose?"

Hadn't his *mamm* or Suzanne told him she'd be here?

"I–I came over to make supper and take care of the girls."

"I see." He sounded resigned.

His lack of enthusiasm dampened her spirits. But his love for his daughters hadn't dimmed. They ran to him for hugs, and then he headed toward Faith. His eyes softened as he neared. His gaze rested on Rose before he held out his arms for Faith, who squirmed away and into her father's arms.

Rose longed for him to embrace her too.

"Time to eat." Hannah's sharp command interrupted Rose's yearning. With a *don't-come-near-us* look, Hannah, with Lillian's help, drained the spaghetti and mixed in the sauce. Then they filled plates for everyone. Neither girl took much spaghetti.

The sharp smell of vinegar permeated the air. Had the girls used it to make the salad dressing?

Pleased they'd both come around to helping, Rose didn't ask. She set out applesauce and the salad, while Joshua seated Emily and Faith.

A homey meal, four children, a handsome man at the head of the table. Rose's dream come true. Except for one minor flaw. Joshua didn't want her in the picture.

~

Joshua had a hard time keeping his gaze off Rose. Her cheeks flushed a shade as lovely as her name. And she'd looked so beautiful, so appealing as she'd stood there holding Faith.

"I sit here." Hannah practically bumped Rose out of the way. His daughter made it clear Rose couldn't sit on his left—in a wife's place.

Hurt flared in Rose's eyes for a moment, but she hadn't intended to sit there. At least he hoped she hadn't.

What had Suzanne been thinking? She'd made this whole

situation awkward. Now Rose expected them to marry. And he couldn't be heartless enough to correct her misunderstanding. He'd talk to Hannah later about her behavior, but maybe his daughter's dislike might discourage Rose from marrying.

After they'd prayed, Joshua took a bite and winced. What was in this sauce? Hannah was studying him, so he tried not to make a face.

"Rose made the meal all by herself," Hannah said. "Me and Lillian just stirred."

Joshua choked down another bite. He appreciated Rose's efforts, but the meal was barely edible. Luckily, she was busy chopping Faith's spaghetti into small pieces and hadn't glanced in his direction.

Hannah took a bite. She coughed and choked and sputtered, spraying her mouthful of spaghetti across the tabletop.

Rose jumped to her feet. "Are you all right? Let me get a cloth to clean up."

While Rose's back was turned, Joshua frowned at Hannah and shook a warning finger for her to be polite. But he couldn't blame her. He'd never tasted so much pepper in spaghetti before. And another sharp taste, almost like pickles. Was it vinegar?

He took a third taste, and his eyes watered. If he married Rose, would they eat meals like this every night?

~

Rose cleaned the mess and smiled at everyone around the table. All the children were picking at their food. Had Hannah talked them into a mutiny?

She lifted a forkful to her lips, trying to appear calm with Joshua sitting at the head of the table. Then she, too, almost spit out her mouthful.

Now the vinegar spill and open pepper container made

sense. Rose raised an eyebrow at Hannah, whose eyes flashed a *don't-you-dare-tell* warning.

Rose had no intention of doing that. "My goodness. I'm so sorry. This doesn't taste at all like my usual spaghetti. It seems as if this batch got mixed up with pepper and vinegar."

Hannah avoided Rose's gaze. Evidently, she had no intention of confessing. But she received a fitting punishment because Joshua enforced the usual Amish rule everyone must clean their plates.

Sadly, they all suffered along with Hannah.

The lemon bars proved to be a hit. Or perhaps everyone was so grateful to soothe their burning mouths.

Rose blinked back tears. By sabotaging the meal, the girls had made it clear they didn't want her around. If Hannah and Lillian disliked her this much and Joshua was still tied to Lena, what hope was there for a marriage?

~

The following week, Joshua helped his parents pack and move. After they were gone, he came to depend on Rose for babysitting and meals. As much as he tried to guard against falling for her, the more time he spent around her, the more she appealed to him.

But Hannah's attitude concerned him. Ever since he'd reprimanded her about the disastrous spaghetti dinner, she'd grown more belligerent and resentful. If she wouldn't accept Rose, how could he consider a marriage of convenience? Now he was torn between hurting Hannah and hurting Rose.

Yet, as the days went by, Faith and Emily clung to Rose, and even Lillian snuggled up when Hannah wasn't looking. If he cut off the relationship, would his three younger daughters suffer?

Finally, Joshua did what he should have been doing all

along. He laid out his concerns, his reservations, and his longings before the Lord. To his surprise and dismay, God seemed to be nudging him in the direction he'd been trying to avoid. For several days, Joshua wrestled with God, but in the end, he sensed the Lord's answer: *Marry her.*

"Rose?" he said one evening after she'd helped him put the girls to bed. "Could we talk?"

His heart thumping an irregular rhythm, he sat across from her in the living room. "You told me you'd prayed about marrying."

She lowered her head and fixed her gaze on her hands. Her nod was barely noticeable.

"I've been praying about it too." He swallowed the huge lump in his throat. "And it seems like God is saying to go ahead."

Rose's head snapped up, but her eyes held wariness.

"It's not that I don't like you or care for you. I do, but—"

"Joshua, I've told you before. I understand."

Except she didn't know all the reasons holding him back. Or the way his past weighed on him. "I don't feel right asking you to marry me. I have so many reasons why I shouldn't. And it doesn't seem fair to you."

Tears shone in her eyes, but she said, "If God's leading both of us in this direction, we should do His will. And don't worry about fairness. Marriage is about giving, not receiving."

But he'd be doing all the receiving. He had so little to give.

~

Rose clung to Joshua's admission that he cared for her. He'd said it in a roundabout way, but his eyes expressed what he hadn't said in words. Caring was a step toward love.

Over the next months, Suzanne and her *mamm*'s enthusiasm

more than made up for Joshua's reluctance. The two of them not only cleaned the house to prepare it for Rose to move in, but they also came to help Rose's family scrub their house for the wedding.

One day, Joshua's *mamm* called Rose into the bedroom. A hand-carved cradle rocked gently near the bed. "My *dawdi* made this for *Mammi*. Then my *mamm* used it for me, and Joshua slept in it as a baby." Joshua's *mamm* hugged her. "I'm looking forward to seeing another grandbaby sleeping in there."

"Shouldn't you give it to Suzanne?"

"Suzanne has everything she needs for another baby. Besides, my grandfather built this house, so the cradle belongs here."

Rose's eyes stung. What a special gift! Her children would use their father's cradle. "*Danke.*" That one word couldn't express all the gratitude in her heart.

~

The day before the wedding, Joshua and his family headed for Rose's house. After the wedding wagon arrived, he helped the men clean the barn and set up benches and tables, while the women decorated the tables. Everything looked beautiful, but Joshua winced at the *eck*. Rose had put flowers on that corner table where they'd sit together as husband and wife.

Tomorrow he'd be a married man again. Was he ready to take on that responsibility? Maybe he should back out now before he caused Rose more heartbreak.

Lord, You know my brokenness and shame. Rose deserves so much better. Nevertheless, not my will but Your will be done.

Peace descended on his soul. Deep inside, when his qualms quieted, Joshua experienced a certainty that God wanted him to marry Rose.

But the next day, as the bishop came to the last part of the wedding service, all those fears flooded back.

The bishop's piercing gaze rest on Joshua. "Do you also have confidence, brother, that the Lord has provided this, our sister, as a marriage partner for you?"

Yesterday, God had impressed on Joshua's heart that he should take Rose as his wife. Pushing aside all the doubts crowding his mind, Joshua choked out a *jah*.

Rose stared up at him, her eyes damp with tears. Had she sensed his reluctance to answer? He hadn't meant to hurt her.

The bishop turned to Rose and asked the same question. "Do you also have the confidence, sister, that the Lord has provided this, our brother, as a marriage partner for you?"

When Rose stole a shy glance at him, Joshua swallowed hard. Then she bowed her head and responded with a shaky *jah*. She trembled as the bishop turned his attention to Joshua.

"Do you also promise your wife that if she should in bodily weakness, sickness, or any similar circumstances need your help, that you will care for her as is fitting for a Christian husband?"

Joshua had failed before, but he prayed he wouldn't do the same with Rose. After a quick request for God's grace and strength, he promised. This time he vowed not to make the same mistakes.

~

After the wedding events ended, Joshua's parents took the four girls with them to spend a long weekend, leaving Joshua and Rose alone together for their first night of married life.

Joshua carried Rose's suitcase into his parents' bedroom, then stood there awkwardly. She glanced up at him with wide, frightened eyes as if waiting for reassurance. If this were a regular marriage, he'd take her in his arms and soothe her fears. Then he'd kiss her and—

She looked so sweet and irresistible. He pivoted before he let his fantasies carry him away. "Well, good night."

He retreated to the attic room where he'd been sleeping since he'd arrived from New York. This had been his boyhood bedroom, the room he'd shared with his brother.

Joshua had turned his back before he could glimpse any pain on Rose's face. He regretted hurting her, but he couldn't take a chance of having more children. Past burdens as well as financial troubles weighed on him. If he couldn't support the family, Rose would also suffer. And he never wanted her to face what Lena had. As much as Rose appealed to him, he must guard against falling for her.

~

Stunned, Rose stared after Joshua long after he disappeared up the stairs. His rejection cut deep into her soul.

For a few agonizing moments during the wedding, she'd feared Joshua would say *neh* to the bishop's question. Had he hesitated because he wanted to back out?

Standing here in the bedroom doorway, she suspected he regretted the marriage. He'd tried to warn her. She'd brushed it aside, believing her love would be enough for both of them.

Because it was a second marriage, the wedding only lasted a half day. Then they'd spent some time with the girls before they left with their grandparents. Joshua had been kind and solicitous the whole time, like a true bridegroom, giving Rose hope for their future together.

Now, waves of loneliness and disappointment crashed over her. Had he been wearing a mask of politeness? Had his tenderness been only a ruse?

Joshua had said the vows to make her his wife, but he

hadn't even stayed with her on their wedding night. Over the past few months, when he'd made it clear this was a marriage of convenience, she hadn't realized he meant she'd spend her nights alone.

In the silent house, Rose lay on one side of the double bed. The cradle sat near enough to touch. With one hand, she reached out and set it rocking.

Would it always remain empty?

CHAPTER FOUR

*S*now flurries the evening before had turned into a blizzard by daybreak. Two feet of snow on the ground meant the outdoor job he'd been about to start had to be postponed. Joshua shoveled the walks and driveway, cared for the horses, and then shut himself in his office in the barn. The small propane heater beside his desk roasted his legs but did little to warm the rest of him.

They'd been married two weeks, and every day proved harder than the one before. His heart leaped every time he saw Rose. Each movement caught his attention. All he wanted to do was take her into his arms. When he wasn't working long hours, he retreated to this freezing office to fight his growing attraction.

Joshua pushed the button on the beeping answering machine. Two *Englischers* had canceled indoor jobs. *Ach*, the rumors must be true.

Last week, one of his crew members had heard gossip about a new *Englisch* business undercutting *Daed*'s company. "They've been spreading lies about you," Stephen had said.

"They're telling people your *daed* was skilled and dependable, but your work is shoddy."

Burying his head in his hands, Joshua gave in to the despair that had been creeping over him for weeks. Winter was hard enough in the construction business. The last thing he needed was to lose more work. Not now, when he'd taken on a wife.

"*Daed?*" Hannah pounded on the door. "Are you coming for breakfast?"

Breakfast? With his stomach churning and his head pounding?

But everyone would wait for him. He stood, opened the door, and took his daughter's hand. Frigid wind hit their faces and whipped their breath into small white clouds.

"I cooked most of the breakfast today." Hannah's rivalry with Rose hadn't abated since they'd married. In fact, it seemed to have gotten worse.

"I'm sure it will be delicious." When she smiled proudly, he teased, "As long as it doesn't have too much pepper and vinegar."

"*Ach, Daed.*" A sheepish smile spread across her face. "But I do cook better than her."

He'd lectured Hannah repeatedly about being disrespectful. And he'd warned his daughter not to call Rose *her*. Right now, though, he had no energy to correct Hannah or to deal with her snits. So he ignored the remark as they hurried toward the back door.

Rose had given Hannah a lot of the responsibility for cooking and playing with the younger girls, while Rose took on the unpleasant chores like diaper changing, cleaning, and scrubbing. The unfair division of jobs bothered Joshua, but he decided to let Rose handle her relationship with the girls in her own way.

Hannah's selfishness underscored Joshua's own guilt. Rose

had taken on all the household chores and bedtime routines while he'd finished a job with a tight deadline. She'd never complained, but he contributed little to their relationship. And now, he might not be able to cover the bills.

Before Hannah opened the back door, Joshua stopped her. He bent down and put his hands on her shoulders. "Since you have off school today, I want you to help Rose with the cleaning."

Hannah thrust out her lower lip, but before she went into a full-fledged pout, he added, "I can count on you, can't I?"

"I'll do it for you, not for *her*," she muttered.

"Rose," he corrected automatically, but Hannah yanked open the door and acted as if she hadn't heard him.

Bacon, eggs, and onions perfumed the air, and the warmth of the kitchen made his icy fingers and toes tingle. Seeing Rose bending over to remove a casserole from the oven made the rest of him tingle. He turned away to hide his reaction.

"That's my casserole." Hannah charged across the kitchen. "I can take it out myself."

Joshua spun around to see Rose step back apologetically.

"I didn't want it to burn," she said softly.

"Hannah!" At Joshua's gruff reprimand, all the children froze and stared at him with wide eyes. He tried to control his next words. "I expect you to be polite and kind at all times."

As Hannah's mouth set, Joshua shook his head. "I also want you to apologize to Rose."

"Sorry, will you forgive me?" Hannah said it so rapidly all her words bumped into each other, and her tone wasn't the least repentant.

But Rose smiled sweetly. "Of course." She handed over the potholders and casserole dish.

"I made this all by myself." Hannah set the breakfast casserole on the table.

RACHEL J. GOOD

"Neh," Lillian corrected, "Rose helped with . . ." At Hannah's furious glare, Lillian stuttered to a stop.

Rose put a hand on Lillian's shoulder. "It's all right," she whispered.

Lillian gazed up at Rose with adoration. Joshua hoped his own eyes didn't reflect the same emotion, but his whole being filled with much more than admiration.

∽

Lillian's darling smile melted Rose. She wanted to hug her new daughter but settled for a gentle squeeze on her shoulder. No sense angering Hannah more.

When she glanced up, she caught a flicker of . . . Was that longing in Joshua's eyes? It disappeared. His neutral expression returned. Rose yearned to peek behind that mask.

She settled into the seat beside him, her rightful place as his wife. A wife in name only. She'd agreed to this marriage, but she'd pictured them laughing together, talking, having fun. Instead, Joshua got more and more distant with each passing day.

After breakfast, Rose stopped Joshua before he headed back out to his office. Usually, she tried not to delay him as he headed off to work, but with the roads still unplowed, he wouldn't be building anything today. She hoped that meant he'd have a little time to talk.

Hugs from the children filled some of Rose's loneliness, but she also craved adult conversation, something Joshua avoided.

"With Christmas coming, could I have a little extra money for presents?"

Shock crossed Joshua's face. "Presents?" he croaked out the word. "I don't think—" He rubbed his forehead. *"Neh,* presents aren't necessary."

Rose didn't mean to have an *Englisch* Christmas with piles

of gifts. She just meant something small and practical. Something to help the girls adjust to life without their *mamm*. And, if Rose were honest, something to help her get closer to the children.

"Just one small present for each girl?" More like a token than a gift.

Joshua turned his back to her. "I said *neh*." His throat hoarse, he added, "The girls don't need gifts. I'd rather they remember it's Jesus's birthday."

He was right. They should focus on the true meaning of Christmas.

Rose tried not to let disappointment color her response. "I see."

~

Do you? Joshua wanted to shout. *Do you know you married a failure? A man so deeply in debt, he'll never escape? A man who just lost three jobs today and who might not be able to keep a roof over your head? A man who's too ashamed to tell you the truth?*

Without turning around, he mumbled, "I have to work."

"I know. I'm sorry I kept you."

The pain in her words stabbed him. *Ach, Rose, it isn't your fault.* He should apologize, thank her for what she'd done, tell her he appreciated her cooking and caring for his daughters, and let her know all the feelings welling up inside each time he looked at her or talked to her.

But if he faced her, he'd be tempted to take her in his arms and—

He slammed a steel door down inside his mind, blocking off those thoughts and emotions.

Joshua opened the back door, and the arctic air froze his body the way his callousness chilled his soul. He couldn't walk away and leave her without telling her at least one truth.

"*Danke* for thinking of my daughters at Christmas." His voice husky, he said, "I'm grateful for everything you've done for them. And for me."

"I enjoy it."

Really? She enjoyed being left alone most of the day and then all night? She enjoyed being married to a man who couldn't even look at her when he complimented her?

One hand still on the doorknob, he made himself say one more thing. "I know this marriage hasn't been easy. It's my fault. I'll try to help out more."

Now that his two main indoor jobs had canceled and the weather had ended his outdoor construction, he'd have plenty of time. The only problem was keeping his feelings in check.

Behind him, Rose's teeth chattered.

"I'm sorry. I didn't mean to make you freeze." He hurried out the door and closed it behind him, locking away the deepest secrets of his heart.

~

Rose stood by the door, shivering as Joshua disappeared into the snow flurries. His words had warmed her inside, but he couldn't bear to look at her as he said them. What did that mean?

He'd only been polite. He might have expressed the same appreciation for an elderly babysitter. Although she'd been sure of it before she married, she questioned whether her love could ever be enough.

Hannah's bossy voice came from the kitchen. "You need to wash the dishes and sweep the kitchen, Lillian. *Daed* said we have to help Rose."

Poor Lillian might end up with all the chores. Rose hurried into the kitchen to intervene. Having all four girls home today would keep Rose's mind from straying to Joshua. At least some of the time.

Hannah glared at Rose as she redistributed the chores. Even Rose's taking over the least desirable ones didn't help. It seemed no matter what she did, she couldn't break through to Hannah's heart. Or her father's.

CHAPTER FIVE

*O*nce the snow melted enough that they could work on the one exterior job, Joshua met his crew at the house. They finished the job, and after he'd received the payment, he gathered the workers together.

"I'm sorry to tell you this, but the two interiors we had scheduled have switched to the new *Englisch* company."

"I told you," Stephen said. "Do we have anything else booked?"

"I'm afraid not." Joshua hated admitting that, especially so close to Christmas. "I'll call when we do." He handed the workers the money they'd earned.

The men headed off, faces glum. Joshua watched them go, his heart as heavy as theirs. He barely had enough money for this week's groceries and no idea when or how he'd get more.

Despite his gloom, watching Rose bustling around the kitchen cheered him. As always, she greeted him with a smile that stirred his pulse.

He emptied his wallet and laid the money on the table rather than handing it to her. He'd learned his lesson the last time he'd touched her. Better not to start that deep desire in his soul.

"*Danke.*" She dipped her head shyly. "I have Sisters' Day this week, and we'll be making and exchanging cookies. We're almost out of baking ingredients. Could I have a little extra for those?"

Rose appeared so trusting, so adorable with her head tilted like that. If he had any money, he'd give her every last penny. But he'd already done that.

Joshua turned away. He couldn't bear to watch her smile fade. "Not this week." The words came out too gruff. He softened them with an "I'm sorry."

Sorry to disappoint her. Sorry he had no more to give. Sorry she'd married him.

~

Rose stood there stunned, staring after him. She'd never asked for anything, not even his time or affection. And he wouldn't even give her a little money?

After he shut himself into the small room where his father had kept his business papers, she picked up the money he'd set on the table. Joshua couldn't even hand the weekly grocery money to her. He went out of his way not to be near her. Could he make his rejection of her any plainer?

Maybe she could cut back a little on groceries so she'd have enough to make cookies. But when she counted the bills, Joshua had given her less than usual. She'd barely be able to feed the family with this.

Emily came over, tugged on Rose's skirt, and held up a picture book. "Read to me?"

"Let me change Faith first."

Rose moved by rote through the diaper changing. She had

to shake off feeling sorry for herself. She had two precious girls to care for and love. They needed her attention.

All three of them headed downstairs and curled up on the couch with four books instead of one. The cleaning could wait until naptime. With one girl cuddled in each arm, Rose struggled to turn the pages. Emily leaned in to help.

Rose thanked God He'd blessed her with these children. They needed her, and their innocent affection filled some of the emptiness in her life.

After a quick knock, the back door opened. "It's me," Suzanne called.

"We're in the living room," Rose said.

Suzanne burst into the room, her cheeks and nose red from the cold. She blew on her gloved hands. "Oh, Rose, you look like the perfect mother. I just knew you and Joshua would be right for each other. Aren't you glad I pushed you both into it?"

Rose focused on the two sweet girls instead of the deeper ache in her heart.

Suzanne never noticed the lack of response. She prattled on. "I told my girls to come home with Hannah and Lillian after school. I hope that's all right. They should be here soon, but I have an appointment this afternoon."

From the glow on Suzanne's face, Rose guessed the news. "Congratulations."

"I'm pretty sure, but it's been so long we wondered if we'd ever have another little one." Suzanne smiled at Rose. "I can't wait until you have a baby too."

Rose forced the corners of her lips up, but her smile wobbled.

Suzanne gave her a sympathetic look. "It might seem like a lot now when you're getting used to four daughters, but I'll be around to help. And Elizabeth Esh is the perfect mother's helper."

Swallowing hard, Rose nodded. She couldn't tell Suzanne

the truth about their loveless marriage. "Is that who you're planning to have?"

That set Suzanne chattering about her future plans and took the spotlight off Rose. Her friend barely paused for breath before jumping to a new topic.

"Have you decided what cookies you'll make for Sisters' Day?"

Rose bit her lip. "I won't be going."

"What do you mean? You have to come. This is our first Christmas as sisters. Well, sisters-in-law."

"I know." She dipped her head and pretended to be engrossed in the page Emily had turned.

Planting her hands on her hips, Suzanne demanded, "Why not?"

"Well, Joshua . . ." Rose couldn't say he wouldn't give her the money. "I'm so busy here . . ."

Suzanne's eyes narrowed. "Is my brother refusing to let you go?"

Before Rose could deny it, Suzanne rushed on. "Where is he? I'm going to give him a piece of my mind."

"He's in there." Rose pointed to the small room off the living room. "But he's working, so please don't bother him. He didn't say I—"

Ignoring Rose, Suzanne marched over, pounded on the door, and burst into the office. The door slammed behind her.

~

Joshua had been poring over his father's records when the door banged open. It crashed shut, shaking the room and rattling Joshua's teeth.

Suzanne, of course.

Until his return to Lancaster, he'd forgotten how forceful his sister could be.

"Why did you tell Rose she can't go to Sisters' Day?" she demanded.

"I don't know what you're talking about."

He didn't have time for his sister's drama. He had more important things on his mind, like contacting some of *Daed*'s former customers to see if they needed home repairs.

"Rose said you're the reason she can't come to our first Sisters' Day together."

Joshua rubbed his forehead. Why did Suzanne have to turn every little thing into a disaster? Had Rose really blamed him? That didn't seem like her.

Oh, wait. She had mentioned cookies for Sisters' Day. She couldn't go because she didn't have enough money for baking?

After all she'd done for him, he couldn't even return one small favor.

"Well, at least you look guilty about it."

"When is it?"

"Next Tuesday."

"Rose can go." Joshua would get the money somehow.

"Good. And why are you sitting in here when Rose is in the living room? You should be out there with her."

Joshua stayed still. He couldn't admit he needed to avoid Rose.

"Newlyweds usually spend all their free time together."

"Suzanne?" His voice rose. "Stop pushing. You pushed me into getting married." Joshua lowered his volume. He hadn't meant to shout at her. "I told you I wasn't ready. And how I live is not your business."

"It is if you're being unfair to Rose."

His voice dropped to whisper. "I'd never do anything to hurt Rose." But he already had. Plenty of things.

⁓

After Suzanne barged into Joshua's office, the back door opened. Four chattering girls entered the kitchen. Rose went out to give them snacks. Three of them greeted her with a smile, but Hannah glowered.

"We don't need you. I can take care of snacks."

"I'm sure you can." Rose tried not to let her hurt show. "I wanted to let—"

Just then Joshua's words "You pushed me into getting married" blasted through the office wall.

Hannah smirked. "Told you."

Rose closed her ears to the rest of the conversation in the office. She turned her head so no one could see the tears threatening to slide down her cheeks.

All the pain she'd been tamping down exploded like shrapnel and pierced every part of her. She'd accepted that Joshua might never love her the way he'd loved Lena, but Rose had assumed he'd made the decision to marry on his own.

The first time he'd come to her house, he'd said he didn't want to marry. Had she and Suzanne trapped him into doing this? Maybe that's why he retreated to the attic every night. He wanted to stay as far away from her as possible.

"My *daed* never should have married you." Hannah dug the barbs in deeper.

Rose fought for control over her emotions, but her voice wavered. "I married your *daed* to help take care of the little ones." Blinking hard, she bent to set Faith at the table.

"We don't need you," Hannah's voice stayed quiet, but savage. "I was doing fine taking care of them without you."

Suzanne breezed out of the office and stopped dead when she heard Hannah's comment. "Hannah, apologize to your new *mamm* right now."

"She's not my *mamm*."

"Your *daed* married her, so she is."

"He didn't want to. He said you made him do it. We all heard him."

Suzanne's face paled. "You heard that?"

Rose didn't answer. She couldn't force any words through her constricted throat.

～

Joshua emerged from the office in time to hear his daughter's statement. If Hannah had heard his comment, then so had Rose. Her stricken face twisted Joshua's insides. He never wanted to hurt her.

"Hannah, you will apologize to your *mamm* and your *aenti*."

"I only told the truth."

Suzanne glanced at the kitchen clock. "*Ach*, I'm going to be late." She hurried out the door.

Hannah's defiant stance made it clear she planned additional attacks on Rose. Rather than taking that chance, Joshua would deal with her later. "Hannah, go to your bedroom. I'll be up later to talk about this."

His daughter stomped up the stairs.

"Rose, I'm sorry." How could words erase the pain he'd caused?

Her eyes downcast, Rose only nodded.

Joshua yearned to take her in his arms and soothe away the sadness on her face. "I'm going to talk to Hannah, and then I need to go out. I'm not sure I'll be back for supper, so please eat without me."

Without answering, she poured milk into glasses and set them in front of each girl.

He headed upstairs to talk to Hannah. Another conversation today that wouldn't go well. Although he understood Hannah's resistance to accepting Rose as her "real" *mamm*, he'd insisted his daughter must be respectful and kind. Hannah might comply when he was around. But he held little hope for a real difference in her behavior unless she changed her heart.

After his talk with Hannah, which had gone as poorly as he'd expected, Joshua returned to the kitchen. Rose stood at the sink with Faith propped on one hip as she taught Emily to wash dishes. Joshua's heart ached. Hannah had been doing dishes alone by age three, but Lena had died before Emily reached that age, so she'd had no one to teach her.

"I'll be back later," Joshua called to Rose.

Her only response was a slight head bob. Until now, he hadn't realized how much her cheerful responses meant to him.

Joshua went outside feeling like a failure as a businessman, a father, and a husband. Tonight might not be the best time for him to miss supper, but he'd come to a decision, and if he didn't do it now, later he might not be brave enough to go through with it.

Forty minutes later, Joshua shivered on Stephen's porch in the biting winds and swirling snow. Yet he hesitated.

Only the memory of Rose's slumped shoulders and downcast eyes forced him to knock. He had to do this for her and for his family.

"Joshua? Come inside before you're blown away." Stephen led Joshua over to the fireplace to warm up.

"You know how you wanted to buy my horse?" Joshua prayed Stephen had been serious.

"You came out in this weather to sell your horse?"

Joshua nodded. "I have another horse I can use." An older plodder he used as little as possible.

"But that horse is special to you."

Very special. And beautiful and well-trained.

Stephen studied him. "When you paid us, did you pay yourself first or last?"

"Last," Joshua admitted.

"So you need money." Stephen didn't ask. He stated it flat out.

If Joshua had waited until morning, he wouldn't have appeared so desperate.

"I'd like to buy the horse." Stephen looked troubled. "But I don't have that kind of money right now, even with my other job. With all of us being out of work . . ."

Before he rushed over here, Joshua should have realized that. He'd only been thinking of Rose.

"Unless you'd consider payments? I could give you a deposit now and pay the rest when I pick up the horse. Maybe in a few months?"

"That'd be fine." Joshua didn't want to sound too eager.

"Hang on. I'll get the money."

When Stephen returned, he counted out bills, and Joshua exhaled a silent, relieved sigh. He had no idea how he'd cover expenses after this month, but right now, he had enough to give Rose extra and to cover this month's bills.

Danke, Lord!

Stephen insisted Joshua stay for supper, and afterward, they discussed some ways to increase business. By the time Joshua returned home, the house had been swallowed by darkness. As he took care of Buddy, the horse nuzzled him. Putting his arms around Buddy's neck, Joshua inhaled the comforting scent of horseflesh.

A lump formed in his throat. "I'm going to miss you, boy."

Buddy had been a huge comfort after Lena died. His horse had filled some of Joshua's loneliness and provided a listening ear for his aching heart. The two of them had developed a close bond, but the lesson Joshua learned then still applied: Hugging a horse didn't fill the yearning for a human embrace.

CHAPTER SIX

*W*ith a heavy heart, Rose stirred the oatmeal for breakfast. Joshua had stayed out so late last night, she'd worried he might not come home. She lay awake until the horse trotted into the driveway. Then she fell into a restless sleep.

If the girls didn't need her, Rose would be tempted to offer to return to her parents' home. Only the promises they'd made at the wedding kept her here. She'd been so sure marrying Joshua had been God's will, but maybe her own dreams and desires had clouded her judgment.

Behind her, Joshua cleared his throat, and Rose jumped. How long had he been standing there?

He set some bills on the table. "Here's the rest of the grocery money and some extra for the cookies. I don't want you to miss Sisters' Day."

Joshua's tone sounded caring, but he had his back to her, so she couldn't read his expression. Had he been working last night? Working to make the money she'd asked for?

"*Danke.*" Joy bubbled up inside at his gift. Perhaps he did have some feelings for her after all.

That happiness stayed with her throughout the weekend, and she hummed as she bundled Faith and Emily into the buggy on Monday morning. Joshua had even smiled at her at breakfast when she thanked him again for the extra money.

Joshua's sisters all hugged her and made her feel welcome. Rose could hardly believe Suzanne had gone from being her best friend to being a sister.

"Look at you," Suzanne teased as Rose helped the little girls take off their coats and boots. "You're glowing. I assume that means my brother made up with you."

The smile almost slid off Rose's face, and she bent to pick up Faith to hide her true feelings. "I'll take these two into the living room to play with their cousins. Be right back."

Before Rose returned to the kitchen, she reminded herself of Joshua's smile this morning. It cheered her. Maybe with time they could have a real marriage.

The day passed quickly with baking and teasing and gossip. Soon everyone packed up the cookies they'd exchanged and headed off to arrive home before their school-age children.

As Rose headed out the door, Suzanne stopped her. "Merilee, one of the girls from the market, is hosting an essential oils party tomorrow morning. Do you want to come with me?"

Rose hesitated. "I have a lot to do. I'm just getting used to caring for the two little ones while Hannah and Lillian are in school."

"Bring them along. Everyone will have their children. They can play like they did today. Some of our buddy bunch will be there."

"All right." For the first time, Rose could attend a get-together without everyone looking at her with pity. Now she had a husband and children.

$\sim$

Joshua set down his fork with a satisfied groan. "That was delicious."

Rose's face shone as she set the plate of cookies in the center of the table after the meal.

Joshua gripped his suspenders to keep from reaching for her. "I, um, guess Sisters' Day was a success."

"*Jah*, your sisters are so nice."

"Except Suzanne." Joshua had meant it teasingly, although Suzanne had a way of getting under his skin. He wished it hadn't slipped out when Rose's smile faded.

Was she remembering the time he'd complained about marrying her? He had to get her mind off that. "The cookies look delicious. Which ones did you make?"

Looking close to tears, Rose pointed to the chocolate chip cookies.

"I'll take two of those. I know yours will be the best."

That brought a slight smile to her face.

Then Hannah said, "I'll take any cookies except those."

Joshua shot her a warning frown. She pressed her lips together.

"I want two of Rose's," Lillian declared.

Hannah muttered, "You would." She shot her sister a mean look.

Lillian looked about to cry. Then she straightened her back. "I like Rose's cookies. And chocolate chip is your favorite."

"It's not anymore." Hannah took two other cookies but looked longingly as Lillian closed her eyes and savored her chocolate chip cookies.

Joshua took a bite of his cookie and made a show of smacking his lips. "Yum. This is the best cookie ever."

Acting as if she didn't care, Hannah bit into her cookie. "What kind is this?" She held it out and examined it.

"Black walnut," Rose answered. "They're a little bitter."

Hannah dropped it on her plate. "You should have told me."

"Would you have listened?" Joshua asked. "Now that you've picked it, you have to eat it."

"That's not fair." Hannah crossed her arms. "Everyone else got better cookies than me."

Joshua raised an eyebrow. "So, you do think Rose's cookies are the best?"

Hannah glowered. She didn't like to admit she was wrong, but it would do her good. "They're not as bad as this one."

"Maybe next time, you'll make better choices." Joshua polished off the last of his cookie. "*Danke*, Rose. That was delicious."

He was rewarded with a huge smile that turned his insides upside-down. Her hand rested on the table, so close he could reach out and—

He pushed back his chair and stood. "I should probably do some more work before bed." His face flamed. He should have chosen a different word.

Rose's teeth clamped down on her lower lip, and she looked anywhere but at him.

He had to change the subject. "Hannah and Lillian, I want you two to do the dishes tonight." It was the least he could do for Rose.

He'd almost reached the back door when Rose said, "I forgot to tell you. Suzanne invited me to an essential oil party tomorrow."

Joshua winced. Lena had enjoyed those, but sometimes she spent too much money.

"You don't want me to go?"

Neh, he didn't. But how could he deny her? She'd done so much for him. "Go and enjoy it."

"You're sure?"

He tried to add more enthusiasm to his voice and expression. "Of course. You work hard. You should have some fun."

He only prayed she wouldn't ask for any money because he'd paid all the bills and had none to give.

~

The next day, Merilee made the party fun with games and refreshments. Then she tried to interest some of them in hosting parties or becoming consultants.

Although the idea intrigued Rose, she had enough to do with four daughters. As several women clustered around Merilee to learn more, Rose headed out to the kitchen for another cup of hot chocolate. She loved the peppermint taste. Merilee had handed out a recipe, and Rose considered buying some peppermint oil so she could make it.

Two of her friends from church huddled together in conversation near the doorway. They stopped talking as she passed and gave her halfhearted smiles. Had she done something to offend them? Or had she only imagined their lukewarm greetings?

Heading back to the living room, she froze when one of the women whispered, "Poor Rose."

Rose stayed just outside the doorway where she could hear, but they couldn't see her, and pretended to sip her hot chocolate.

"This time of year is always hard in the construction business. And now that Joshua laid off Abe, I'm not sure what we're going to do."

"Maybe Abe could apply at Clement Construction. They've taken all Joshua's contracts."

"Stolen is more like it. I feel sorry for him."

"Me too. He came to the house the other night and sold Stephen his horse. Stephen gave Joshua some money and promised to pay the rest when we can afford it."

Trembling, Rose leaned against the wall. Was that why

Joshua had been so upset over Christmas gifts? And why he'd given her less grocery money than usual?

She thought he'd worked for the money he'd given her for cookies, but instead, he'd sold his horse. He loved that horse. Had he done that for her?

"Rose, are you all right?"

At Suzanne's sharp question, the women stopped talking.

"*Neh.* I don't feel well. Could you get Emily and Faith for me?"

"Sure." Suzanne grinned and waggled her eyebrows. "You're going to be joining me?"

Rose shook her head. She'd never have a baby.

The news about Joshua had shaken her. Why hadn't he told her? After she got both girls down for a nap, she could barely concentrate on cleaning or planning supper.

A little after three, Hannah burst through the back door and stormed up the stairs. "This is all your fault," she yelled.

Lillian came up behind Rose. "Don't mind, Hannah," she whispered. "Her dress tore at recess, and everyone laughed at her."

"*Ach*, no. Did it catch on something?"

"*Neh*, it split when she jumped up for a fly ball." Lillian's eyes filled with tears. "Hannah only has one school dress that still fits. Now that it's torn, I don't know what she'll wear."

Rose had been so busy getting settled in as a wife and mother, she hadn't paid much attention to Hannah's clothing. She'd stayed away from interfering in Hannah's choices, but she should have noticed that.

She hurried upstairs and tapped on the doorjamb. "Hannah, if you give me your dress, I'll mend it."

Hannah's pillow muffled her words, but there was no mistaking her anger. "Go away and leave me alone. I can sew it myself."

At suppertime, Hannah came down in the old dress she wore when cleaning. That, too, was tight and too short.

Rose wished she'd paid closer attention. Lena must have made those dresses more than a year ago. Hannah had grown a lot since then. The other girls had Hannah's hand-me-downs, which were stored in a big box in the closet. But Hannah had nothing new to wear.

If only Rose hadn't spent the money for the cookie ingredients. She could have bought fabric instead.

After the girls went to bed, she tiptoed upstairs to check on them. Hannah had fallen asleep, a flashlight still shining on the bed beside her. A needle glinted in its dying beam. Rose picked it up along with the dress Hannah had been stitching. The threadbare material puckered around a lumpy seam.

Poor Hannah. Rose's heart went out to her. Losing her *mamm* and trying to take on all her mother's duties must have been difficult.

After easing the dress material from under Hannah's arm, Rose headed to the living room, where she turned on the propane lamp and unpicked Hannah's stitches. If Hannah tried to put this dress on tomorrow, the seams on the other side would rip out.

After opening the other side seam, Rose resewed the dress as close to the seam edges as she could. That would give Hannah a little more room, but she really needed a new dress. Rose let the hem down as far as she could.

With Joshua out of work, how could she get Hannah a dress?

~

Joshua came in from his office in the barn, relieved that he'd lined up two small jobs. They'd barely make a dent in next month's bills, but he appreciated having work. He only wished he could call his crew back too.

A light flickered in the living room as he crossed the kitchen. Had Rose gone to bed, leaving the light on? They couldn't afford to waste propane.

Joshua rushed through the doorway and skidded to a stop. Rose, her pretty profile illuminated by the soft glow, sat sewing.

"Joshua? Are you all right?"

"I thought someone left the lamp on."

"I'm sorry. I need to mend Hannah's dress."

"I see." Couldn't she do it during the day? He held his tongue. He shouldn't criticize when she was doing so much for all of them.

And he struggled to even think about propane when all he wanted to do was take her in his arms.

CHAPTER SEVEN

*A*fter Joshua left early the next morning, Hannah flounced into the kitchen, her expression sullen. "Why did you touch my dress? I wanted to do it myself."

"I worried you might not have time."

Hannah's chin wobbled. "But *you* shouldn't have touched it. My *mamm* made this." Hannah rushed from the room and out of the house without stopping to put on a coat.

Rose hurried to the window to keep an eye on her as she crunched through the snow in stocking feet, flung open the barn door, and ran inside. "Lillian, can you take Hannah's coat and boots to the barn?"

Lillian got ready and rushed after her sister. Minutes later, she trudged back to the house, her face solemn. "Hannah's hugging Buddy and won't look at me. I think she's crying."

"Did she put on her coat and boots?"

"*Neh.* I left them there."

Rose prayed Hannah would use them.

Tears trembled on Lillian's eyelashes. "After *Mamm* died, *Daed* held me when I cried, but Hannah wouldn't let him. She cried in the barn with Buddy. *Daed* did too."

Ach, how lonely they must have been with only a horse for comfort.

Rose hugged Lillian and then fed everyone breakfast. Hannah stalked off to school without eating or waiting for Lillian, but at least she'd put on her coat and boots. Lillian ran after her with their lunches.

Sighing, Rose cleaned up the kitchen. After Faith went down for her morning nap, Rose smoothed out her newest dress on the floor. She'd made it before the wedding and had only worn it once. Then she laid Hannah's ragged everyday dress on top as a pattern but cut generous seams and an extra deep hem. The leftover material could make a new dress for Faith.

Rose squeezed sewing between chores, lunch, and naps. Hannah stomped to her room after school. Rose fed the other girls a snack, then took two chocolate chip cookies and the dress upstairs. Hannah kept her face buried in the pillows, but her heaving shoulders revealed she was crying.

Rose set the plate on the bedside table. "Here's a new dress that might fit better."

Hannah, her face red and tear-stained, flung the dress across the room. "I don't want that. Or your cookies."

If only Rose could comfort Hannah, but she rejected anything Rose tried. *Lord, please wrap Your loving arms around her.*

Rose left the room, shutting the door quietly behind her.

The next morning, Hannah, her face defiant, came to breakfast in her usual dress, but after she had her coat on, she raced upstairs. "I forgot something."

When she came down, the hem of Rose's dress peeked out from under her coat. And when Rose went upstairs, the cookie plate had been cleaned of every crumb. Hannah's old dress had been tucked under her pillow.

Poor Hannah. She must miss her *mamm* so much.

Rose headed for the farmer's market with the two younger girls. First, she stopped at Suzanne's stand.

"What are you doing here?" Suzanne demanded after she hugged all of them.

"I want to talk to Merilee about doing essential oil parties."

"How come?"

Rose didn't want to reveal Joshua's money troubles, so she asked, "Does Joshua believe in giving Christmas gifts?"

"You want to make money for Christmas? What a good idea!" Suzanne turned to her husband. "I'm going with Rose."

When he nodded, Suzanne joined them. "Joshua usually gave each of the girls a book or a small toy."

"I want to make dresses for the girls."

"That would be perfect. Joshua's so lucky to have you." Suzanne's self-satisfied smile reminded Rose that Joshua had been trapped into marriage, and she frowned.

"Are you worried about what to give Joshua?"

"*Neh.*" Although she had no idea what to get Joshua. Or even if she should give him anything. If she had the money, she'd pay Stephen back for the horse.

Once they reached Merilee's stand and heard the price of the demo kits, Rose's plans nosedived. If she'd listened to the rest of Merilee's presentation yesterday, she'd have known the cost.

"I see." Rose turned to hide her disappointment and almost bumped into an elderly woman wobbling on her cane.

After clutching Rose's arm to steady herself, the woman glanced up. "Are you all right, dear?"

The woman's sympathetic eyes made Rose long to spill everything troubling her.

"So, Rose," Merilee asked, "which demo kit do you want?"

Rose kept her head turned and bit her lip. She couldn't afford any of them.

"Wait, Merilee." The woman studied Rose. "You want to be a consultant, don't you?"

"*Jah*, but—"

"Fine. Give her the biggest kit, Merilee. I'll pay if this young woman agrees to do a party at my house next week."

Suzanne whispered to Rose. "That's Mrs. Vandenberg. She owns the market. You have to say *jah*."

"You will do that, won't you?" Smile lines crinkled around Mrs. Vandenberg's eyes.

"Of–of course."

"Perfect. Next Wednesday at eleven o'clock?"

"*Jah*," Rose agreed, "but I can't let you pay."

"I already did." Mrs. Vandenberg fumbled in her purse and pulled out a card. "Be there at ten-thirty so we can talk."

Rose took the card from the woman's trembling hand. "I will."

"You're so lucky." Suzanne squeezed Rose's hand as Mrs. Vandenberg hobbled off. "She's really rich, and she loves to help people."

Her first demonstration for a rich *Englischer*? Rose gulped.

"I'll take care of Emily and Faith," Suzanne offered as Rose fingered the card. "I don't know how she'd feel about having children in her fancy house."

"Merilee," Mrs. Vandenberg called over her shoulder, "this may be your best Christmas ever. Yours too, Rose."

If only that were true, but with Joshua and Hannah both ignoring her, her husband's business in ruins, and little chance of winning her husband's love, Rose suspected it might be the worst Christmas ever.

⁓

Over the next week, Joshua wondered as Rose slipped off immediately after the girls went to bed and locked herself in the bedroom. Strange clinking and rustling came through the door along with some lovely smells.

If they had money, Joshua might suspect Christmas surprises. But he'd made it clear they wouldn't give gifts this year. Rose had agreed, hadn't she?

She also seemed nervous and distracted during the day, barely noticing him or smiling when he came into the house. After wishing she'd stop giving him those appealing smiles that set him ablaze, now he longed for her attention. He tried to tell himself this was for the best, but his spirits plummeted.

She still made meals, cleaned the house, and took care of the girls. But now she didn't seek his approval at mealtime or even seem to hear his compliments. He'd thanked her several times for last night's hot chocolate with peppermint. Instead of hanging on his every word, she'd nodded and retreated to the bedroom.

He took several Christmas cookies from the jar, wishing he could get the former Rose back. Not that he deserved that after treating her so coldly. She probably felt like this whenever he ignored her.

He longed to apologize, but she gave him no chance. She didn't even meet his eyes anymore.

~

Usually a woman talked with her husband before taking a job, but Rose kept her essential oils a secret. She met with Merilee several times for training when Joshua wasn't home, and Rose slipped into the bedroom frequently to practice. Guilt built inside until she couldn't look at Joshua.

Mrs. Vandenberg's party loomed larger and scarier. What if she did everything wrong?

Rose took the girls to Suzanne's early Wednesday morning and headed to the outskirts of Lancaster. When she pulled into the mansion's driveway, she gulped. After tying the horse to a lamppost, she stood on the porch to gather her courage before banging the lion's head knocker.

Mrs. Vandenberg opened the door and led Rose into an interior more elegant than the mansion's stone façade. Her throat tightened. She'd never be able to speak to the women gathered here.

While Rose set up, Mrs. Vandenberg inquired about Rose's children, husband, and her life. Without meaning to, Rose ended up answering the prying questions truthfully. And what she didn't say, Mrs. Vandenberg seemed to sense.

"Construction work is hard to find this time of year, isn't it?" she asked.

Rose nodded.

"Has Clement Construction cut into your husband's business?"

How did this elderly woman know so much?

Mrs. Vandenberg laughed. "People are always surprised that at ninety-two I still keep up with everything going on in the community. I believe God gave me money to assist others, so I need to watch for opportunities."

So that's why she helped me?

"I went to Merilee's stand that day because the family's struggling to pay their daughter's hospital bills. She's too proud to accept money, so I asked God for a way to help her, and you were my answer to prayer."

And Mrs. Vandenberg had been the answer to Rose's prayers. "I still want to pay for my kit."

"You can take it out of whatever you earn today."

Ten minutes later, Rose stood in front of twelve *Englisch* women. She bumped her display table and samples rolled off and landed on the thick Persian rug under her feet. She prayed none of them had leaked.

"It's all right, dear," Mrs. Vandenberg said quietly. "Elaine will pick them up. You go ahead with the presentation."

The games and activities that had been fun at Merilee's party seemed too silly and childish for these sophisticated ladies. Rose's voice shook as she launched into the demonstration.

"If you just pass around some samples," Mrs. Vandenberg suggested, "I'm sure everyone here will want some oils for themselves and for Christmas gifts. They know it's going for a worthy cause."

Rose's face heated. *Her or Merilee? Or both?*

A few ladies asked questions, but most bent their heads over the order forms. They seemed to be scribbling rapidly.

After everyone enjoyed the refreshments Mrs. Vandenberg's cook set out on the sideboard in her elegant dining room, each lady took out a checkbook or cash. Rose had never seen so many hundred-dollar bills in her life.

"Ines and Millie enjoy having parties," Mrs. Vandenberg said. "I'm sure they'd be happy to book them before the holidays."

Both ladies looked startled, but nodded.

Another woman approached Rose. "These little bottles are so cute. Maybe I should buy them as favors for my daughter's wedding. I'd like her to select the scents, though. We'll need about five hundred."

Five hundred times the cost of each bottle just for wedding favors?

Ines booked her party, and then added, "My charity helps underprivileged women earn income. I'll take information for them about becoming consultants."

Rose left the party dazed. One lady purchased forty of the largest gift packages for a women's luncheon, and Mrs. Vandenberg, in addition to a large personal order, had added a corporate order for Christmas gifts for everyone in the farmer's market and another for her charity staff.

Had she talked her friends into single-handedly paying off Merilee's bill? Even if only a small percentage of the sales went to Rose and Merilee, they'd both make a lot of money. And Rose had made more than enough to pay back Mrs. Vandenberg.

Rose was late getting home, and Hannah had already started supper. She waved off Rose's offer to help.

"I don't need your help," Hannah said through gritted teeth.

Even Hannah's attitude couldn't blunt Rose's happiness. They'd have money for groceries, Christmas gifts, and paying off Joshua's horse. Best of all, Rose had another gift for Joshua. Mrs. Vandenberg wanted to talk to him about a construction job starting after Christmas. Rose planned to give him the business card on Christmas morning.

~

When he came back into the house two hours after supper, Joshua grumbled to himself as he headed into the living room to turn off the light. They'd soon run out of propane, and he had no money for more. Why was everyone so careless?

"Could you leave the light on a little longer?"

Rose? He hadn't noticed her, but once his eyes adjusted to the dark, he made out her shadow in the wingback chair, which had been turned so the light fell over her shoulders.

"Do you need it?" He could have kicked himself. Why had he growled that as if she'd done something wrong?

"I'm hemming Hannah's dress for the Christmas program. Her teacher wants them tomorrow."

"Oh." In his scramble for new construction jobs, he'd forgotten the program was next week. He turned the light back on. "*Danke* for doing that. And for the meal tonight. Chicken pot pie is one of my favorites."

"I know."

She'd made it for him? He moved into the living room so he could see her face. "That was nice of you."

Her needle slowed. Then stopped. She lifted her head, and her eyes glowed as if his words meant the world to her. How starved for affection and attention she must be if that simple comment meant so much.

Tonight, she'd reverted to the sweet, caring woman he'd married. Whatever had caused her to be so distant last week had ended, but he still ached inside at being ignored. Rose must experience that loneliness every day of this marriage. Joshua regretted his self-centeredness.

He sat across from her as she sewed, and his heart swelled with love. He wished he could express all the feelings hidden in his heart.

"Rose, I—"

She glanced up at him, and he couldn't speak. With every fiber of his being, he longed to take her in his arms, hold her close. He closed his eyes. But blocking out the vision of her loveliness did little to assuage his desire.

What could he say?

"I'm glad I married you." *Except for the temptation.*

"You are?"

He didn't blame her for acting skeptical after he'd spent so much time avoiding her. Gripping the chair arms to keep himself in place, he opened his eyes and looked deep into hers. "*Jah*, I am. I couldn't ask for a better wife and mother for my girls. You deserve a better husband. It's just that—"

Rose held up a hand. "No need to apologize. I understand. You explained it all before we married." Her tender smile almost proved his undoing.

She lowered her eyes and concentrated on the needle, but not before the flame of hope he'd kindled in her eyes had been doused by sadness. A sadness he had no way to erase.

CHAPTER EIGHT

*J*oshua's admission touched Rose's heart and gave her hope. He'd never love her the way he did Lena, but his words of appreciation wrapped her in a soft, warm blanket. She comforted herself with them when she lay alone in the dark next to the empty cradle.

The following week at the school Christmas program, they sat together and their arms brushed, sending sparks through Rose. This was the closest they'd been since their wedding day. Several times, she closed her eyes to concentrate on Joshua's nearness, his breathing, his strong hand inches from hers.

Each time Hannah or Lillian said their parts, he smiled at them and then at Rose. Her breath caught in her throat at the look in his eyes, and her anticipation built. Maybe tonight he'd take her into his arms.

After the program, he helped put the children in bed, something he'd been doing more often the past few weeks. When he turned to her, she melted under his gaze. He took a step toward her, his arms outstretched.

Then his eyes squeezed shut, and his hands dropped to his sides. When he opened his eyes, they were shuttered and bleak.

Rose turned before he could see her distress. "Goodnight," she mumbled and hurried downstairs.

She slept that night with one hand on the cradle and her cheek against a damp pillow.

When she woke, she resolved to stop hoping for more in their relationship. Each time she did, Joshua dashed her dreams. Instead, she threw herself into work, scheduling several parties. With Christmas coming, people seemed eager to buy gifts, especially the *Englischers*. None of the parties compared to Mrs. Vandenberg's, though.

Over the next week, Mrs. Vandenberg's friend Ines signed up twenty women who wanted to sell essential oils, and her charity paid for their kits. From the money Rose made from the new consultants' sales, the other parties she'd scheduled, the wedding order, and Mrs. Vandenberg's multiple orders, Rose bought Christmas candy, extra cookie ingredients, and material to make dresses for the girls. She also repaid Stephen for the horse and explained it was a Christmas surprise, so he wouldn't tell Joshua.

Every spare minute when the girls weren't around, Rose cut out and sewed the dresses. As she finished each one, she wrapped it in striped paper and hid it in her closet. Before they wed, she'd told Joshua marriage was about giving, not receiving. She focused her energy on giving to Joshua and the children to ease some of the pain of her unrequited love.

~

After almost giving in to holding Rose on the night of the Christmas program, Joshua reined in his runaway feelings. He only complimented Rose when the children were around. They'd prevent him from starting anything he'd regret.

With less than a week until Christmas, nobody wanted home renovations, so he worried about paying the bills. He was grateful when the bishop introduced him to Sam Miller and his family, who'd be moving into the rundown farmhouse across the road that weekend.

"We could use some help with repairs," Sam said as they shook hands.

"I'd be happy to do whatever you need. I'll also be over on Saturday to help you move."

Joshua hummed on the way home. He had no idea if Sam planned to pay him, but Joshua had time on his hands, so he'd be glad for something to do.

That night at supper, he announced the news. "An Amish family with three children bought the farm across the road. I told the bishop I'd help them move on Saturday."

Rose's forehead wrinkled. "They're going to live in that old place? It's been vacant for years."

"It definitely needs work, so I'll go over after Christmas to help."

"That's nice of you." Her smile made him feel like a hero.

Except he wasn't a hero. A hero would have a job and be worthy of his wife's love.

"We can all help them move," Rose said, "and we'll have them over for supper."

Thunderclouds gathered on Hannah's face.

Before his daughter could spoil Rose's plans, Joshua changed the subject. "They have a girl your age, Hannah. You'll have a friend nearby."

"What if I don't like her?"

"I'm sure you'll like Sari. She seems nice." He turned to Lillian. "Their other daughter, Annie, is a year younger than you and is in a wheelchair after an accident. They also have a baby."

Lillian beamed—unlike Hannah, who scowled.

But on Saturday, Hannah made friends right away, and Lillian hung back, shy and hesitant. By suppertime, though, most of the furniture had been put in place, and all four girls giggled together.

Joshua had plenty of chances to check out the dilapidated house. It needed major repairs. If he had to choose where to start, he'd pick the old summer kitchen attached to the back of the house. Getting that ready to use would take a lot of work.

During the day, Rose and Maddie had taken turns caring for the two little ones. As they ate supper, Rose offered to put the baby to sleep while Maddie directed the placement of the last few pieces of furniture.

When Joshua mounted the stairs, he almost dropped the dresser he was carrying. His heart thumped double time at the sight of Rose in the rocker with the baby. The tenderness in her face as she gazed down at the sleeping infant made Joshua ache for her. She deserved to have children.

He shook his head, trying to block out old memories threatening to overwhelm him. But as hard as he tried, he couldn't erase the image of Rose cradling a baby.

~

Two days later, on Christmas Eve, Emily and Faith were sleeping, and Joshua and Rose had just tucked the two older girls into bed when a loud explosion rocked the air.

Hannah bolted upright. "What was that?"

Rose rushed to the window. Flames shot from the summer kitchen of the Millers' house. She prayed they were all in another part of the house.

After a quick glance, Joshua dashed from the room. "I'll call 9-1-1 from the barn and then go over to help."

Rose raced downstairs after him and slid on boots. Maddie might need help with the girls.

Hannah pounded down the stairs behind her. "I want to come too."

"Grab some blankets," Rose said. "They probably won't have coats. But be careful and stay out of the way of the rescuers."

She raced across the road. Flames licked at the roof of the summer kitchen. Black smoke spiraled into the sky. The roaring fire illuminated the darkness, casting flickering light on Maddie as she struggled to maneuver the wheelchair off the porch. Sari grasped the footrest to help.

"I need to get the baby," Maddie cried. "Rose, can you help with this?"

"Where's the baby? I'll get her."

"Asleep on the living room floor."

As she ran, Rose fumbled to untie her apron. Then she bent and scooped up snow. She darted up the porch steps and through the doorway.

Burning wood spit and crackled as the rest of the kitchen whooshed into flames. Smoke billowed toward her. Panic clawed at Rose's insides. Fire ate along the walls behind her and flared up the stairs to her right. She dodged shooting sparks.

Go left. The living room was to the left off the hallway.

Acrid clouds of smoke choked her. Stung her eyes. Heat seared her skin. She pressed the wet apron to her face. The snow had turned to slush. Frigid water dribbled down the front of her dress.

She had to find the baby. Where was the doorway? She felt along the wall until her hand bumped into the door jamb. At last!

Rose dropped to the floor and crawled to stay below the haze. She ran her hand along the hot, rough boards until she felt the edge of a quilt. She tugged it toward her, praying the baby hadn't inhaled too much smoke.

The baby squalled as Rose wrapped her in the icy wet apron. *Gut!* She was still alive. Rose tucked the kicking, squirming bundle close with one arm and pressed the damp edge of the apron over her nose and mouth. Then stooping low, she raced for the door, keeping her upper body arched over the baby to protect the little one from falling debris as the smoke curled lower. Grit and ash drifted down around her.

The kitchen roof caved in, spraying a shower of sparks. Fire consumed the side wall, heading toward the front door. Rose had to get out before the house collapsed around them in a fiery explosion.

~

Joshua raced across the street. Hands pressed to their mouths, Hannah and Lillian stood on the edge of the lawn, staring in horror at the flames. A pile of blankets lay at their feet. Rose wouldn't have let them come over here by themselves, would she? But where was she?

He knelt in front of his daughters, blocking their view of the burning house. "Don't look at the house. Let's take the blankets over to Maddie and the girls. They're shivering."

Maddie, her hands clenched and teeth chattering, stood near the porch, her daughters on either side. All three of them had their heads bowed in prayer.

Joshua hated to interrupt them, but he needed answers. "Where's Sam? Where's the baby? Where's Rose?" The questions spilled from his mouth.

"Sam went to town." Maddie's face paled. "Rose, she . . . she . . ."

"She what?"

"Went in for the baby."

Joshua stood stock still. Rose was inside that burning inferno?

"*Neh*, Joshua, don't go in." Maddie clung to his arm. "Your girls need you."

He couldn't leave Rose in there. He shook free of Maddie's clawlike grasp.

Hannah shrieked, dropped the blankets she'd been passing out, and grabbed at his pant leg. He removed her hands and set them in Maddie's.

"Hold Hannah back, Maddie."

Sirens whirred in the distance. The firefighters were on their way. Thank the Lord!

He had to save Rose. He sprinted through snowdrifts.

Behind him, Maddie pleaded, "Come back, Joshua, come back . . ."

Before he reached the house, flames whooshed across the lintel above the door. It crashed down, blocking his way.

And trapping Rose inside.

CHAPTER NINE

*J*oshua yanked at a rotted post in the porch railing. With a loud splintering, the wood pulled free. Sparks showered around him. He slapped at the ones that landed on his sleeves. Using the post, he dragged the flaming beam from the door. Inch by inch, he tugged it to the edge of the porch.

The wooden post caught fire. Joshua plunged it into the snow. The end sizzled. Crumbled into ash.

Sparks landed on his hat. He tossed that into a snowbank.

Paint blistered on the porch's wooden floor boards. The wood smoldered.

With one final heave, he rolled the blazing beam into the snowdrifts. Steam hissed from the melting snow.

He mounted the porch steps two at a time. Then stopped. *Rose!*

Pressing one end of her apron to her soot-covered face, she crouched in the doorway, a black-wrapped bundle in her arms. Coughing and choking, she stumbled toward the porch.

"Wait!" Joshua shouted. She couldn't cross the smoldering boards. They might catch her hem on fire.

She stared at him with wide, frightened eyes.

He tossed mounds of snow in front of her. The snow sputtered and puddled. "Walk through the water."

When Rose neared the edge of the porch, Maddie rushed over and unwrapped her baby daughter from the apron. *"Danke, danke, danke . . ."* She hugged the bawling baby against her.

Reaching up, Joshua lifted Rose and carried her a safe distance from the fire. Then he lowered her to the ground, but kept his arms wrapped around her. He never wanted to let her go. Icy wetness penetrated his clothing. But it couldn't compare to the ice in his heart at the thought of losing Rose.

Earsplitting sirens deafened him as the fire trucks and ambulance raced up the driveway. Flashing lights strobed around them, coloring the snow red. A man with a bullhorn barked out orders. Firefighters unwound hoses and worked to contain the fire.

Joshua shivered, but not from the cold. Smoke fumes choked him as he bent close to Rose's ear and whispered, "You could have been killed." He couldn't bear the thought. All the love he'd denied flooded through him. She was so precious to him. If she'd died in there, he'd never have had a chance to tell her what she meant to him.

"Rose, I—"

An EMT knelt beside him. "We need to check her out."

Not now, he wanted to shout. Not when he'd finally gotten the courage to admit his feelings. He'd made a terrible mistake. He had to fix it.

~

Rose snuggled close to Joshua as adrenaline drained from her body. Too weak and exhausted to move, she rejoiced in leaning against his broad, firm chest, her head against his rapidly thumping heart. She didn't want to sit up or move.

Although she could hardly focus with Joshua's arms still wrapped around her, Rose complied with the EMT's instructions.

After the EMT checked her over, he addressed both of them. "Keeping that wet cloth over your face helped, but watch for these symptoms." He rattled off a list.

Rose hoped Joshua was paying attention, because her mind kept drifting to the warmth of his body, the tenderness of his arms.

The EMT suggested other remedies that Rose barely heard. Then he asked, "Do you have any cough drops or hard candy?"

Rose nodded. The girls' Christmas candy. "Peppermints," she croaked.

"Good. They'll soothe your throat if it's dry or sore. Get plenty of sleep if you're weak or tired. Propping your head on pillows will make it easier to breathe."

Joshua, his voice husky, responded, "I'll take good care of her."

Rose blinked back tears at his tenderness.

After the EMT left, Joshua said, "We should get you home." He helped Rose to her feet and kept an arm around her, supporting her.

Lillian and Hannah dashed toward them. Lillian flung her arms around Rose and her *daed*, hugging their legs.

Out on the road, Sam's horse galloped at breakneck speed toward the house. The firetruck and ambulance blocked the driveway. A neighbor rushed over to take the reins, and Sam jumped from the buggy.

"Maddie!" He embraced his wife. Then he hugged his daughters. "Thank the good Lord you're safe."

Joshua motioned across the road. "Put the horse in our barn," he told the neighbor.

"And you can all stay at our house," Rose offered.

Sam stared at the smoking ruins. "Joshua, can you stay to help?"

Joshua hesitated and glanced down at Rose tenderly. "I want to be sure my wife is all right."

Reluctant to lose his protective arm around her, Rose wanted to beg him to stay with her, but she couldn't be selfish. "Go with Sam. I'll be fine."

When he released her slowly, Rose missed the warmth of his arms. She wanted to watch him, but she had another family to care for. As she led everyone across the road, Lillian clung to her hand. Hannah hung back, but her usual sullen expression had been replaced by anxiety.

"Don't worry," Rose told her. "Your *daed* will be careful. He won't go near the fire."

"I know." Hannah bit her lip.

When they got to the house, Rose sent Maddie upstairs to get her family cleaned up. Then she washed Lillian's hands and face at the kitchen sink. "Can you get a nightgown of yours and one of Hannah's for the girls?" Rose glanced at Hannah for confirmation.

"*Jah*, they can have one of mine." Hannah's eyes filled with tears. "They won't have any clothes or anything."

"Perhaps you can share some of your books and games. And maybe some clothes in the hand-me-down box will fit."

"Faith's baby clothes are in the bottom. *Mamm* made them before . . ." Hannah turned her head away.

"Lillian, could you check for something for the baby to wear?" Rose asked.

Her face somber, Lillian nodded and climbed the stairs.

Rose turned back to the sink. "I'd better wash my hands before I get a nightgown for Maddie." After she finished, Hannah, her eyes sad and faraway, still stood there.

Rose wanted to embrace her, but the stiff set of Hannah's

shoulders showed a hug would not be welcome. So, Rose waited—and prayed—for the young girl who was facing deep pain.

Hannah twisted her hands in front of her. "You ran right into that burning house. You could have been killed."

"I didn't have time to think about that. The baby needed to be rescued."

"Yes, but if I'd been in there . . ."

"If you'd been in there, nothing could have stopped me from charging in, because I'd never want to lose you."

"Even after all I've done?"

"*Ach*, Hannah. I know it's been hard for you, having a stranger come into your house and into your *daed*'s life."

A tear trickled down Hannah's cheek.

"And even before that, you took on caring for all the younger girls. That's a lot to handle when you've lost your *mamm*. You probably didn't even get to cry."

"H—how did you know?"

"I've seen how strong you've been for all of them."

Hannah burst into sobs.

Rose took a chance and held out her arms.

Hannah hesitated, then she ran over, and shoulders heaving, buried her face against Rose's dress. Rose stroked the soft blonde bedtime braids cascading over Hannah's shoulders as she sobbed.

After a while, Hannah lifted her head. "*Phew.* Your dress stinks."

Rose smiled. Hannah would always be Hannah. "And you have soot all over your face. Come on." Rose held out her hand.

For a moment, Hannah stared at Rose's outstretched arm suspiciously. Then she reached out tentatively and let Rose take her hand. Together, they went to the kitchen sink, and Rose gently wiped the soot and tears from Hannah's face with a wet towel.

"Can you help me get the bedroom ready for Sam and Maddie?" Rose asked.

Hannah hesitated. Rebellion flashed in her eyes.

When she set her jaw, Rose prepared for a refusal. Without waiting for an answer, Rose pivoted and started for the bedroom. Tentative footsteps followed her.

"What's that?" Hannah asked when she entered the bedroom.

"Essential oils." Rose had set up a display on the dresser top so she could practice her spiel. "Can you pack those in here?" She handed Hannah a box with slots.

"What are they for?" Hannah lifted each small vial and set it in place.

Rose didn't want to tell Hannah before she'd confessed to Joshua. "I'll tell everyone tomorrow." If they had any time alone. They'd have company for quite a while until the Millers could rebuild their house.

She rummaged through her drawer for her nicest night-gown and then opened her closet to select aprons and two dresses for Maddie. She'd forgotten about the Christmas packages hidden inside. The top one tumbled to the floor.

Hannah picked it up and studied the tag. "For me?"

"It's for tomorrow."

She squeezed the paper. "What's in it?"

"You'll have to wait until tomorrow to see." Rose reached for the package, but Hannah held it out of reach.

"Wait." Gently, Hannah detached the tag with her name on it. "You can give it to Sari."

Rose's heart swelled with pride. "Oh, Hannah." Rose placed her hand on Hannah's shoulder and squeezed gently, marveling that Hannah didn't shrug her off.

A silent song of praise filled Rose's heart. She'd made a breakthrough with Hannah. If only she could do the same with

Joshua. After his gentleness tonight, it would be hard to go back to the coldness of their usual relationship.

Once everyone had cleaned up and the children were dressed in nightgowns, Rose tucked the two youngest under the covers. Faith shared Hannah's bed; Lillian and Emily slept in the other.

Lillian wrapped an arm around Rose's neck. "Hannah told me about the presents," she whispered. "Please give mine to Annie."

Rose swallowed the lump in her throat. What sweet, giving daughters she had.

When Rose peeked into the other room, Annie had fallen asleep, but Maddie and Sari sat with their backs against the wall. Maddie had one arm around Sari and the other cradled the baby. Maddie looked exhausted.

"Here, let me take the baby," Rose offered. "I'll put her to sleep."

"*Danke.*" With distraught eyes, Maddie handed over the baby and hugged her oldest daughter.

A few nights ago, Rose had helped Maddie put the baby to bed. Now, she'd put the little one to sleep again. Only this time in the cradle. Rose's eyes stung as she wrapped a quilt around the sleeping baby. The cradle wasn't empty anymore. But it held someone else's child.

CHAPTER TEN

*B*y the time Joshua and Sam returned, hot and sweaty and covered in soot, the children had all fallen asleep. Maddie, after thanking Rose multiple times, had put on the nightgown and slipped into bed.

Joshua directed Sam upstairs, and like Rose had done earlier, he did a quick wash up at the kitchen sink until Sam finished.

"They lost pretty much everything," Joshua whispered. His eyes reflected deep grief. "I'll be right back. I need to get Sam some clothes to wear."

When Joshua returned, he asked, "If Maddie and Sam are in your bedroom, where will you sleep?"

"On the couch."

"That's too uncomfortable."

"I don't mind."

"I know you don't, but I do. You can sleep upstairs in my bed."

"Then where will you sleep?"

"With you." He glanced at her as if unsure of her response. "If that's all right?"

All right? She'd been longing for that since the day they were married. She couldn't meet his eyes. And she couldn't confess the joy brimming inside. "*Jah*," she said softly.

~

Once he'd washed up and everyone was asleep, Joshua crawled into bed. He longed to pull Rose close, but after the way he'd treated her, would she welcome his touch? She'd let him hold her earlier, but she'd been dazed.

"Rose?" He touched her shoulder, and she stirred, moving closer.

Dare he hope?

When he reached for her, she came willingly. She smelled of peppermint. He wrapped his arms around her and pillowed her head on his chest, inhaling the smoky aroma still clinging faintly to her hair. "*Ach*, Rose, I thought I'd lost you."

How could he have been so foolish? He'd lost Lena because of his neglect. Now he'd almost driven Rose away by a different kind of neglect.

She snuggled close to him, and his eyes stung. This time it wasn't from the smoke. He didn't deserve her kindness and forgiveness.

"Rose?" he whispered against her ear. "I need to tell you something."

"Can it wait until tomorrow?"

"I guess," he mumbled. He wanted to explain, to confess, to make things right. But she'd been through an exhausting evening. He could wait.

"I'm sorry." Rose rolled over to face him. "I'm tired, but not too tired to listen to you."

As always, she thought of others first. She had such a giving heart.

"I need to tell you about Lena."

Rose's eyes glinted in the moonlight. Tears? She closed them before he could tell, but she winced. He hadn't meant for this to be as painful for her as it was for him, but he needed to tell her the truth.

"I'm sorry I've been so cold to you. From the first day I saw you again, I fell for you. Ever since, I've been fighting not to take you in my arms."

She fixed her eyes on his face as if testing the truth of his words.

"As much as I wanted to, I couldn't. I shouldn't. First, my business may close. I don't have enough money to pay bills."

"I know."

"You do?"

She nodded. "I wish you'd shared that with me."

How long had she known? Who'd told her? But Joshua didn't want to get sidetracked. "That's why I didn't want another baby. It's also why I didn't want to marry. Not because I didn't love you. I do. With all my heart."

Rose, her face filled with hope, hung on his every word.

He'd denied her so much. How could he ever make it up to her?

"But the real reason I didn't want to marry is because of what happened with Lena. She wasn't feeling well, and money was tight, so I asked her to wait to go to the doctor." Joshua's voice broke. "By the time she went several months later, she was pregnant. When she got the cancer diagnosis, she refused treatment."

"*Ach*, Joshua."

"She died a month after Faith was born. If I'd let her go to the doctor . . . if she hadn't gotten pregnant, she might not have died. It's all my fault."

"Don't blame yourself." She sat up and set her hands over his. "God has a plan. You have to trust Him."

"Rose, I can't let anything happen to you. I want to protect you, take care of you." He enfolded her in his arms and cradled her close to his heart.

~

Tears streamed down Rose's cheeks. The Lord had blessed her beyond anything she'd ever dreamed. All those years of wishing she'd had a husband, God had been saying, *Wait. I have the perfect man for you.*

"You're crying?" Joshua brushed away the teardrops with a gentle fingertip.

"Happy tears." She sighed. "*Ach*, Joshua, I've loved you for so long, and I thought you'd never love me."

If she'd trusted God and left the future to Him, she could have saved herself years of heartache. And all the pain of the last few months.

Joshua's arms tightened around her. "I'm sorry for hurting you like that."

But that was all in the past. Rose wanted to stay in the present.

Present reminded her of presents. She needed to tell Joshua what she'd been doing. Drying her tears, she gazed up at him shyly. "I have a confession to make."

Worry entered his eyes.

"I should have discussed this with you first, but I'm a consultant for essential oils."

His brows drew together. "What does that mean?"

"That I'm selling essential oils, thanks to Mrs. Vandenberg."

"The wealthy charity lady?"

"You know her?"

"I know about her. Stephen suggested I contact her. She constructs buildings all over the county and fixes up houses for the homeless."

"Mrs. Vandenberg gave me her card. She wants you to contact her after Christmas."

Joshua pulled back and stared into her eyes. "Are you serious?"

After she nodded, he drew her close again and rested his chin on her hair. "You're amazing, Rose King."

Rose King. The first time he'd called her by her married name. She blinked back tears because she had more to tell him.

"I made enough money to pay the bills, make a gift for each of the girls, and"—she hoped he wouldn't be upset—"I paid Stephen back for the horse."

"You did what?"

"That's my Christmas gift to you. I hope you don't mind." She peeked up at him.

"Mind? Rose, I don't know what to say." Joshua's expression changed from stunned to sad. "But I don't have anything for you."

"You've given me the most wonderful gift of all." When he looked puzzled, she added, "Your love."

He gave her a fierce hug, then his arms around her gentled. "You deserve that and so much more."

But Rose was content with what she had. Mrs. Vandenberg had been right when she'd predicted this would be the best Christmas ever.

~

The next morning at breakfast, Hannah appeared in her old, threadbare dress, one hand tucked behind her back. The dress Rose had made for her was draped over her other arm. "Here, Sari," she said. "This is for you."

Then Hannah pulled three gift-wrapped packages from behind her back. Two were smoothly wrapped. The other was lumpy and covered with tape. She handed them to Sari, Annie, and Maddie.

Maddie's mouth quivered as she watched the girls open their gifts of new dresses. Then she opened the package of baby toys Faith had outgrown. "*Danke.* I wish I had something to give all of you."

"You don't have to give us anything," Hannah said. "It's more blessed to give." But she looked longingly at the dress Sari had unwrapped.

Joshua smiled at Hannah, then whispered in Rose's ear. "She learned to be giving from watching you."

"I have more material. I'll make Hannah and Lillian dresses after Christmas," she said quietly.

Over the next few weeks, the Amish community came together to rebuild the house and the ramshackle barn and sheds with materials supplied by Mrs. Vandenberg. And after Joshua spoke with her, she put him in charge of buying and rehabbing houses for the homeless. Plenty of indoor work for him and his crew. He'd even have to hire on new workers.

Donations of clothing, furniture, and household goods showed up every day on their front porch until Maddie and Sam had more than enough to furnish their house. Maddie helped Rose sew dresses for all the girls, and they shared the cooking.

Rose spent her days humming and looking forward to time spent with Joshua. Her heart pitter-pattered whenever he walked in the door and a special look passed between them. Her pulse raced whenever he brushed past her, often on purpose. A thrill passed through her whenever he reached for her hand when they were alone.

But falling asleep in his arms at night was the highlight of every day. Waking in the morning, often Rose didn't open her eyes, afraid the joys of the previous night had been only a dream. But then Joshua stirred beside her, his breathing deep and even, and she delighted in the truth that his love was real.

On the day the Millers moved into their brand-new house, Maddie smiled apologetically. "*Danke* for all you've done. We're sorry for putting you out so long."

"It was our pleasure." Joshua smiled down at Rose.

At the look in his eyes, her soul overflowed with joy. The Millers hadn't put them out. They'd brought them together. If it hadn't been for the fire, she and Joshua would still be living like strangers. God had used the fire to work a true Christmas miracle.

Joshua waited until Sam and Maddie crossed the street before closing the door. As soon as they were alone, he drew Rose close. She wound her arms around his neck, and they shared a kiss. A kiss that took her breath away. A kiss that revealed the depth of his love. A kiss that held so many promises for their future.

THANK YOU FOR READING
THIS BOOK

I'm grateful you chose it. I pray the stories uplifted and blessed you. **If you enjoyed these stories, I hope you'll read my Amish novels.**

Website: http://www.racheljgood.com
Amazon: https://www.amazon.com/Rachel-J-Good/e/
B019DWF4FG
Facebook: https://www.facebook.com/racheljgoodnovels
To learn more about the Amish, join the Hitching Post:
https://www.facebook.com/groups/196506777789849/
And if you haven't already, you can sign up for my newsletter
at http://bit.ly/1qwci4Q

ABOUT THE AUTHOR

USA Today bestselling author Rachel J. Good writes life-changing, heart-tugging novels of faith, hope, and forgiveness. She grew up near Lancaster County, Pennsylvania, the setting for her Amish novels. Striving to be as authentic as possible, she spends time with her Amish friends, doing chores on their farm and attending family events.

Rachel is the author of several award-winning, bestselling Amish series in print or forthcoming – *Love & Promises, Sisters & Friends, Unexpected Amish Blessings,* and *Surprised by Love,* along with two books in *Hearts of Amish Country* – as well as many anthologies, including *Amish Christmas Twins* and *Christmas at the Amish Bakeshop* with Shelley Shepard Gray and Loree Lough. She is also the coauthor of the *Prayerful Author Journey: Inspirational Weekly Planner.*

Rachel hosts the Hitching Post, an online site where she shares Amish information and her book research. She also enjoys meeting readers in person and speaks regularly at book events, schools, libraries, churches, book clubs, and conferences across the country.

Find out more about her at:

Website: http://www.racheljgood.com

Facebook: https://www.facebook.com/racheljgoodnovels

Twitter: https://twitter.com/RachelJGood1

Goodreads:https://www.goodreads.com/author/show/ 14661177.Rachel_J_Good

Pinterest: https://www.pinterest.com/racheljgood1/

Bookbub: https://www.bookbub.com/authors/rachel-j-good

Instagram: https://www.instagram.com/rachelj.good

Amazon: https://www.amazon.com/Rachel-J-Good/e/B019DWF4FG

Newsletter sign-up: http://bit.ly/1qwci4Q

Hitching Post: https://www.facebook.com/groups/196506777789849/

ALSO BY RACHEL J. GOOD

Have you read them all?

~

SISTERS & FRIENDS series

Change of Heart

When her younger sister goes wild during *Rumschpringa* and dates an *Englischer*, Lydia Esh teams up with his older brother to break up the couple. But she doesn't count on falling for an *Englischer* herself. Will Lydia stay true to her faith if it means giving up the man she loves?

Buried Secrets

Emma Esh has recovered physically from the accident that almost claimed her life, but she has no memory of the year before the accident, so she has no idea why her sister tries to keep her from falling in love with their next-door neighbor Sam Troyer. But an unexpected visit from an old boyfriend and the gradual return of her memory tears Emma's life and romance apart.

Gift from Above

Sarah Esh's peaceful life is torn apart when a parachutist crash-lands on her family farm and begs her to keep his presence secret because his life's in danger. That promise tangles her in a web of deceit that endangers innocent people, ruins her best friend's reputation, and tears apart the Amish community. Sarah must confess and repair the damage she's done, but how can she admit the truth to Jakob Zook, knowing it will end their relationship?

Big-City Amish

After Abner Lapp's betrayal and his choice to leave the Amish community, Rebecca Zook tries to forget him, but how can she ignore his mother's plea to watch his four young brothers during her cancer treatments in New York City, even if it means being around Abner? Rebecca's tender heart won't allow her to ignore him when he's hurting, but she can't let herself fall for him again, especially when he's not right with God.

~

LOVE & PROMISES series

The Amish Teacher's Gift

A teacher at the Amish school for children with special needs, Ada Rupp struggles to balance her job with caring for her seven orphaned siblings. She has no time to date, but she'll do anything in her power to help her young student, Nathan Yoder, and his grieving widowed father.

The Amish Midwife's Secret

When Amish midwife Leah Stoltzfus insists on using herbal remedies for her patients, sparks fly between her and the new *Englischer* doctor, Kyle Miller. In more ways than one. Can they overcome their differences to rescue a pregnant teen and save her unborn baby?

The Amish Widow's Rescue

After Grace Fisher's husband dies unexpectedly, her neighbor, the reclusive Elijah Beiler, offers to help with her animals and household repairs just to be neighborly. He has no intention of getting entangled with the pregnant widow or her children; he's been hurt enough in the past. But he hasn't counted on Grace's young son, who's determined they need a new daddy.

~

UNEXPECTED AMISH BLESSINGS series

His Unexpected Amish Twins

When Micah Miller becomes the guardian of his twin niece and nephew after their parents are killed in a buggy accident, he's grateful for Hope Graber, owner of a horse therapy farm, who helps all three of them all deal with their grief. Hope makes them smile again and wins a place in Micah's heart. But will his deep-seated fears and Hope's close partnership with her *Englisch* trainer keep them apart?

His Pretend Amish Bride

Priscilla Ebersol has no chance of marriage after her boyfriend's humiliating rejection ruins her reputation, but after she helps an Amish camel farmer in a nearby town and she's mistaken for his wife, Priscilla's matchmaking *mamm* sees this as the perfect opportunity. Unfortunately, her meddling might drive the couple apart instead of together.

His Accidental Amish Family

Following a buggy accident, Anna Flaud is told she'll never walk again. She refuses to accept that and spends years recovering, and she's also working toward becoming a foster parent. Then she's offered a chance to fulfill her dearest wish—motherhood—by adopting three siblings with special needs. But it comes with strings attached: she needs a husband. Her exercise therapist, Levi King, would be perfect for the role except Levi can't trust himself to care for one child, let along three.

~

SURPRISED BY LOVE series

Unexpected Amish Proposal

After Fern Blauch loses her market stall, Gideon Hartzler offers to share his stand with her, but once they start working together, will her rival in business end up as a rival for her heart?

Unexpected Amish Courtship

Isaac Lantz, who trains Labrador retrievers as guide dogs, is enamored with Sovilla Mast, who sells homemade dog food and treats. Gaining a dog's affection is easy, but bashful Isaac has no idea how to win the heart of the woman he loves.

Unexpected Amish Christmas

To help himself recover after a buggy accident, Jeremiah Zook pens inspirational letters to grieving families mentioned in the Amish newspaper. Moved by the letter he's sent, Keturah Esch corresponds with him. Little does she know, Jeremiah has a nearby market stand. When he shows interest in her, she rebuffs him because her heart belongs to the anonymous letter writer. A Christmas gift accompanied by a letter might just hold the key to both their hearts' desires.

Amish Marriage of Convenience

When widower Stephen Lapp moves his five children from New York State to Lancaster County, Pennsylvania, his only plan is to buy his family's farm stand. But on Stephen's first trip to the market, his brave act of kindness nearly ends in catastrophe—until strong-willed Nettie Hartzler saves him—and makes an impression he can't forget. Nettie has no interest in getting involved with any man. But when Nettie runs into serious money worries and Stephen proposes a marriage of convenience, she's distressed and conflicted. She's come to know Stephen's gentle heart and generous soul, but will he marry her if she reveals her dark past?

Her Pretend Amish Boyfriend

Noah Riehl has dark secrets in his past that prevent him from marrying a faith-centered Amish girl like Caroline Hartzler. But when she needs a fake boyfriend to discourage a persistent suitor, who won't take no for an answer, he agrees to rescue her. But will his kindness lead him into the very relationship he's vowed to avoid?

Dating an Amish Flirt

Everyone accuses Rachel Glick of being a flirt because she's caused several breakups and broke many hearts, but she only wants to spend time with her brother's friends after his death. Josh Yoder wants to help the grieving family, and God seems to be leading him to Rachel. But with her history of breaking hearts, is she the right choice?

Missing Her Amish Boyfriend

Anna Mary Zook is struggling to cope with her new job at the market and care for her five younger siblings as Mamm spirals into another depression. Abe King longs to be there for her, but he can't leave his aging father to run their New York state farm alone. Can Abe and Anna Mary find a way to be together?

∼

ANTHOLOGIES

Amish Christmas Twins, Christmas at the Amish Bakeshop, Amish Christmas Kinner (with Shelley Shepard Gray and Loree Lough)

Amish Christmas Miracles, More Amish Christmas Miracles, Amish Spring Romance (with Jennifer Beckstrand, Jennifer Spredemann, and others)

Amish Across America (free; with multiple authors)

Amish Christmas Cookie Tours (with Mindy Steele and Jennifer Beckstrand)

Love's Truest Hope (with Mary Alford and Laura V. Hilton)

Love's Thankful Heart, *Plain Everyday Heroes*, *Love's Christmas Blessings*

(with Laura V. Hilton and/or Thomas Nye)

∾

NOVELLAS

Amish Christmas Treasure, *Amish Mistletoe & Miracles*, *Amish Wedding Day Revenge*, *Amish Twin Trouble*, *Missing Amish Daughter*, *Amish Secret Identity*, *Amish Thanksgiving Strangers*

∾

OTHER TITLES

Amish Quilts Coloring Book (regular and large-print versions)

Prayerful Author Journey: Inspirational Weekly Planner

Hearts Reunited in *Hearts of Amish Country series*

Love's Secret Identity in *Hearts of Amish Country series*

Check for more Rachel J. Good titles here.

Made in the USA
Monee, IL
28 September 2025